and grinned. 'OK, well zen can you take a messaaarge? Tell 'im . . . 'e stink!'

Dad slammed the phone down and cackled. 'Now we play the waiting game!'

Since his latest humiliation at Demento's, it seemed Dad Dread had once again spiralled into a mania of plotting and planning, his head whirling with evil schemes. He was pleased that Danny was finally home. He thought a fresh mind was what was needed to come up with something spectacularly diabolical. He was about to be disappointed.

'What do you mean you have no ideas?' he said. 'What do they teach you at that school, anyway?'

Danny couldn't think of anything to say. He loved his dad, but he was kind of full-on.

'OK,' said Dad with an exhausted sigh. 'Let's watch a little TV, see if that will help.'

Danny blew out through his lips. Most kids love TV, but not him. Not when the lair only had one channel: World News.

OXFORD
UNIVERSITY PRESS

Great Clarendon Street, Oxford OX2 6DP
Oxford University Press is a department of the University of Oxford.
It furthers the University's objective of excellence in research, scholarship,
and education by publishing worldwide in

Oxford New York

British Library Cataloguing in Publication Data

Data available

ISBN: 978-0-19-274263-6
1 3 5 7 9 10 8 6 4 2

Printed in Great Britain
Paper used in the production of this book is a natural,
recyclable product made from wood grown in sustainable forests.
The manufacturing process conforms to the environmental
regulations of the country of origin.

By the Brilliantly Funny **BEN DAVIS**

HILARIOUS!

Featuring the most embarrassing dad on the planet

RIDICULOUS super-villains,
and *OUTRAGEOUS* evil plans

Perfect for fans of *Despicable Me*
and *The Incredibles*

Try before you buy with this funny extract from Danny Dread.

The Dread lair was built into the side of a mountain. It wasn't the most state-of-the-art compound in the world, but still had all you needed for a basic super-villain set-up—aircraft launch bay, laboratory, transmission room with a giant screen, and camera for making threatening videos, that kind of thing.

Danny threw on some clothes and clomped down the grand, stone staircase into the lab. Dad stood behind his desk, dialling the Dreadphone. He hopped from foot to foot with bags the size of hammocks hanging beneath his eyes.

'What are you doing, Dad?'

'Starting World War Three!' Dad whispered. 'Now, shhhh.'

Danny chuckled to himself and sat down in a swivel chair with Earl in his pocket. He wasn't too worried about this one.

''Ello,' Dad said in the worst French accent ever heard by human ears. 'Is zis ze White 'Ouse?'

Danny spun around in his chair and looked up, watching the cave ceiling twirl.

'Could I speak to ze prrresident of ze United States? Zis is ze prrresident of Frrrrance.' Dad winked at Danny

DANNY DREAD

BY THE BRILLIANTLY FUNNY

BEN DAVIS

OXFORD
UNIVERSITY PRESS

Chapter One

Danny Dread was the latest in line of the dastardly Dread clan of super-villains.

♟ great-great-grandson of Artemis Dread—creator of the ghastly pox which popped its victims like over-inflated balloons

♟ great-grandson of Polonius Dread—evil genius behind the trillion-dollar World Bank robbery of 1901

♟ grandson of the fearsome Phileas Dread—kidnapper of royalty and renowned as the most dangerous, deadly, and disgusting man the world had ever seen

♟ son of Larry Dread—inventor of the Super MegaExplosionRay* and the everlasting deadly volcano.**

Yes, Danny Dread, a boy with generation after generation of evil coursing through his veins, a boy with hatred etched into his very soul...

...wouldn't even hurt a fly.

* which didn't work
** which stopped erupting after a week

Usually when people say that, they mean it as a figure of speech, but in Danny's case, it was actually true.

It was his last class of the school year at Demento's Academy for Young Evil Geniuses—Applied Superhero Torture. They'd been building up to it all year, designing instruments of death and destruction for the sole purpose of subjecting a superhero—the evil genius's natural enemy—to the most painful end possible. Danny had secretly hated every moment. And now, when he actually had to flip the switch and sizzle the poor little fly that was the superhero substitute, he just couldn't do it.

'What are you waiting for?' squawked his teacher, Dr Viscera. 'Finish the job!'

Danny's hand hovered over the switch. One flick would produce a tiny laser, which would burn its way up the plinth the fly was strapped to, and slice both in half. He had practised many times with bits of rock and fluff, but he knew there was no way he could go through with it with a living being.

'What's the matter, Dread? Scared?' said Rufus Exploso—head boy, and voted Most Likely to Conquer

Earth in the Name of Evil three years in a row.

Danny tried not to let them see he was shaking. He glanced at his friends, the twins, Murray and Matt Mayhem, but they just looked embarrassed.

'Danny Dread, if you do not liquidate that fly immediately, you will fail this entire module. Do you understand?' Viscera barked.

'I can't,' said Danny in a tiny voice.

The rest of the class jeered and hooted.

'Why not, boy?'

Danny's knees trembled. 'I don't know, I just can't.'

The jeers got louder.

'By the fires of Hell!' said Viscera. 'These are the basics. Class, tell Dread what he needs to lose.'

'HIS CONSCIENCE,' the class shouted in unison.

'Because what is an evil genius with a conscience?' said Viscera.

'WEAK.'

'And what use do we have for the weak in the League of Evil?'

'NONE. NONE. NONE. NONE.'

'Can't believe you wouldn't kill that fly,' said Murray as they filed out of class. 'You're such a wuss.'

'Shut up, Murray,' said Danny. 'You didn't kill yours either.'

Murray snorted. 'Well, that's because I forgot to connect my torture device to any electricity, but if I had . . . KABOOM!'

Matt chuckled. 'Yeah, right.'

'Well, at least I didn't use an expander ray instead of a destructor one,' said Murray. 'Your fly is as big as a cat now.'

They rounded the corner into the hall, where the school motto shone down from above the window.

DEMENTO'S ACADEMY FOR YOUNG EVIL GENIUSES—DO AN EVIL DEED A DAY.

Danny hated that motto. In the entire twelve years of his life, he'd barely managed a single evil deed. He did once ride his bike through a puddle too quickly, which slightly splashed the trouser leg of an old man, but that was it.

'Thing is, I actually meant to make the fly massive, so the death would be extra gory,' said Matt. 'I would have done it too, if it hadn't escaped.'

Murray shook his head as if to say, 'Yeah, right,' and smoothed down his moustache. He had been trying to grow that thing all year but had barely managed two hairs. Still, it was his pride and joy.

'Exploso is such an idiot,' said Danny. '"What's the matter, Dread? Scared?"'

Danny said it in a perfect Rufus Exploso voice. The twins loved it. It was his top talent. He could do everyone from Dr Viscera to the groundsman, Polyp. Of course, it wasn't so funny when Polyp heard him and chased him with a rake, but that's the trade-off when you have the gift of impersonation.

Matt cackled. 'That sounded just like Exploso,' he said. 'What a moro—' He never got to finish the word because he was too busy hitting the floor with a loud bang. Rufus Exploso had stood on the back of his cape and nearly strangled him.

'What did you do that for?' Matt rasped as he got to his feet.

'You lot are pathetic,' said Rufus. Even though he was only three feet tall, he still managed to be intimidating. But that was the Explosos all over—what they lacked in height, they made up for in wickedness.

Danny said nothing and stared at his shoes. It was true— the three of them didn't exactly look that forbidding—the Mayhem twins in their matching capes and Danny all tall and gawky, with his hair that never quite sat right, and his tie that never quite stayed in the middle.

Rufus and his cronies—the much bigger Race Trenchfoot and Maximus Blackheart—circled the three boys.

'I mean, at least these cape idiots try to be evil,' said Rufus, pointing a tiny finger at them. 'But Dread,' —Rufus shook his head as if he were looking at a pitiful kitten he was about to run over with a lawnmower— 'Dread doesn't even belong at this school.'

Rufus was trying to get a reaction out of Danny, but it wasn't going to work. Danny agreed with him—he didn't belong there.

'I mean, your father is a sorry excuse for a super-villain. Everything he does ends in failure,' said Rufus. 'The only reason you're here is because of your grandfather. You bring shame upon his evil name.'

'Hey!' Murray yelled. 'No he doesn't!'

'Yes, he does,' a voice came from behind them. They turned around and there, on a shelf in the Evil Wall of Fame display, was Phileas Dread himself—the scourge of the free world. Or rather, the scourge of the free world's head, preserved in a glass jar.

'Oh, hello, Granddad,' said Danny.

'Don't "hello, Granddad" me, you little slug,' said Phileas. 'Seeing you, a proud Dread, being pushed around by an Exploso is a disgrace.'

Danny normally tried to hurry past his granddad's

spot but today, thanks to Exploso, he couldn't avoid him.

'He failed Applied Superhero Torture, sir,' said Rufus. 'He wouldn't even kill a fly.'

'Wouldn't kill a fly?' Phileas furiously bobbed in the preservation fluid. 'When I was your age, I'd already enslaved half of Europe. You don't deserve the name Dread. Oooh, if I still had a body, I'd come down there and give you what for.'

Danny walked away, followed by Rufus and his minions. He didn't want them to see him getting upset. It was difficult for him to explain how he felt. It was as if he'd been born into the wrong life. Like a cow being born as a fish. He'd want to moo and produce milk, but all he'd be able to do would be to swim and do those really long poos.

The Mayhem twins tried to catch up but Maximus and Race grabbed them by their capes and bounced them up and down like yo-yos. Before Danny could get away, Rufus jumped up and snatched his bag off his shoulder.

'Let's see what's in here,' he said with a sneer. 'Maybe cute puppies, or flowers?'

'Give that back, Rufus,' Danny growled as scarily as he could. 'I'm warning you.'

'Dread is warning me,' Exploso said. 'How funny.'

Rufus reached into Danny's bag and pulled things out—a pencil case, calculator, textbook on diamond robbery techniques—until he found what Danny really didn't want him to find.

'What's this, then?' said Rufus.

He held up a book in his tiny hands. It had **TOP SECRET, KEEP OUT** scrawled across the front in huge black letters, which only made him more curious.

Danny lunged and tried to grab it, but Rufus was too slippery for him. Danny could not let Rufus see what was in there. If anyone found out, Danny would be history. Not even the Mayhems knew.

Rufus dropped the bag so he was just holding the book. 'What could be in this that you're so ashamed of?' he said. 'Do you write . . . poetry?'

'No,' said Danny. 'Just give it back.'

Rufus's mouth twisted into a smirk. 'How much do you want it?'

Danny shrugged, trying not to look bothered. 'I don't. It's nothing anyway.'

Rufus grinned. 'Then you won't mind if we take a look...'

'NO!' Danny made another grab which only made the tiny tyrant's smile bigger.

Rufus spotted something in the distance behind

Danny. He reached into his pocket and pulled out a sickly sweet. Within two seconds, Matt Mayhem's giant mutant fly had landed on his hand. Its weird tongue shot out of its mouth and began dissolving the sweet. This was a big fly by anyone's standards, but when held by the miniscule Rufus Exploso, it looked enormous.

'If you want your book back so badly, you'll kill this fly,' said Rufus.

Danny's mouth dropped open. If he couldn't kill a normal-sized fly, he wasn't about to harm a giant one. He looked into its enormous eyes and his stomach twisted like a pretzel.

'I won't do it,' said Danny.

Rufus tutted. 'There's that conscience again, Dread. You know what Dr Viscera told you about that.'

He whistled at Race, who had just finished hanging Matt up on a hook by his cape. 'Bring me the implement.'

Race nodded and pulled a pointy wooden stick the size of his forearm out of his bag. He passed it to Danny. It felt cold and heavy in his hands.

Danny knew he couldn't kill the fly, but if Rufus looked in that book, it would mean disaster. He stared at the ground and tried to think of a way out.

'We haven't got all day, Dread,' said Rufus.

Danny touched the end of the spike. It was sharp. He knew he was going to have to do it.

'Hey!'

A voice from behind jolted Danny out of his thoughts. He turned around and there was the head teacher of the Academy, Dame Demento. With her long grey hair and fierce green eyes, she had been known to make even the evillest outlaw tremble.

'What is going on here?' she snapped. 'Is this bullying?'

Rufus looked at Race and Maximus, then back at Dame Demento. 'Yes, ma'am.'

Her dry old face cracked into a big smile. 'Excellent. Keep up the good work.'

With that, she clicked her heels and carried on down the corridor.

'Anyway,' said Rufus, who by now had the fly in a firm grip, as it frantically buzzed to try and escape, 'no time like the present.'

'You might as well do it, Danny,' said Murray, swinging on his hook. 'Show everyone you're not scared.'

Danny closed his eyes and took a deep breath. With his hands grasping the base of the wooden stake, he knew what he had to do. It wasn't pleasant, but, he had to admit, Murray was right.

He raised it high, then quickly changed direction and smacked Rufus on the head with it. Rufus stumbled backwards and released the fly. Race and Maximus dived at Danny, but he dodged them and they butted heads, ending up in a heap on the floor. Danny took advantage of the confusion by grabbing his book and running away to his room.

'Only a couple more hours until I go home,' Danny said to himself as he barricaded his door. Then he saw a note on his desk that made his heart sink.

PARENTS' EVENING—LAST DAY OF TERM

Chapter Two

Demento's Academy for Young Evil Geniuses lay in an undisclosed location, perched on the edge of a giant cliff, surrounded by jagged rocks, in the middle of a dark and stormy sea, that swarmed with horrendous monsters. No one could possibly escape alive.

At the end of term, the parents of the budding evil geniuses would come and pick them up in their deadly super-villain aircraft. And while they were there, the teachers would fill them in on how diabolical their little devils had become.

Danny stood on his chair and peeped through the bars of his window. Planes swooped down on the island like colossal bats, blocking out the early evening sky.

He sat on his bed and sighed. If there was one thing he hated more than school, it was Parents' Evening. He thought about trying to escape, but the three-hundred-foot drop into the mouth of a megalodon didn't seem particularly appealing.

Parents' Evening was always a drag because it just showed how much of a disappointment Danny was to his dad. He tried to be evil when he was younger, but he couldn't stomach it. It was as if he were allergic—just like Murray Mayhem was allergic to nuts. The only difference was, evil didn't make Danny's head swell to the size of a blimp. It just made his insides churn.

At the back of the top-secret book were some drawings: complex sketches of masks and capes and lightning-fast cars; drawings that revealed Danny's darkest secret—a secret that would get him expelled from the Academy and even worse, destroy his father.

Danny Dread wanted to save the world.

He didn't know when it had started—it was probably when he was playing with his toy ray gun in the lab at home, watching his dad cook up a plan to fire Venus into the sun. Even at an early age, the idea of such senseless destruction broke his heart. He wanted to be the one to stop it—or rather, his alter ego, lovingly sketched in the back of his top secret book: Mynah Boy!

Mynah Boy could be the one to do it. Danny had chosen that name because the mynah is a bird that can mimic sounds perfectly, just like he could. He thought he could somehow use that ability to stop evil. He wasn't sure how, but details could be worked out later.

Danny was about to add some colour to Mynah Boy's gloves when he heard a knock. In a panic, he opened his wardrobe and threw the secret book inside.

'SON!'

Standing in the doorway, in his tatty old overcoat, with his hair sticking up on top of his head in crazy tufts, was his father, Dad Dread.

He swept into the room with a huge smile on his face. He moved quickly for someone who looked like they were constructed entirely from meatballs.

'How you've grown, my boy!' he yelled. 'Tell me, what awful atrocities have you committed this term? Have you blown up a nunnery?'

'Um, no.' Danny scratched the back of his head.

'Did you unlock the cages of all the man-eating animals at the zoo?'

'No.'

'Oh ho ho!' Dad wagged his finger. 'You must have done something truly abominable! No, don't tell me, let me guess . . . Did you put a chemical into the water supply which made everyone go crazy and start eating each other's BRAINS?'

'No!'

Dad's smile shrivelled up. 'Oh. Well, what did you do?'

Danny shrugged. 'Um, some things. General . . . evil stuff, you know?'

Dad smoothed his tufts down only for them to spring back up instantly. 'Hmm,' he said. 'Let's see what your teachers have to say.'

Chapter Three

DEMENTO'S ACADEMY FOR YOUNG EVIL GENIUSES

REPORT

Applied Superhero Torture — **F**
Failed to kill fly.

Blast Ray Gun Target Practice — **F**
Failed to shoot cut-outs of little old lady and woman with pushchair.

Instruments of Death — **F**
Plane wouldn't fly because it didn't have wings. Or an engine.

Bank Robbery — **F**
Let all the hostages go and wouldn't even steal a pen on a chain.

'I don't understand it,' said Dad. 'It can't be how I raised you. I always taught you never to say please and thank you, to talk with your mouth full, and to have nothing but contempt for your fellow man. What went wrong?'

Danny didn't know what to say. He felt awful.

'Mr Dread . . .'

Dad gulped. Dame Demento stood in front of them, her bony hands on her hips. She seemed even scarier than she did when he was a pupil at the Academy.

'Y-yes, Dame Demento, ma'am.' He went to take his hat off, but realized he wasn't wearing one, so stole one from the head of a passing child, before putting it on and taking it off again.

'I don't think I need to tell you how disappointed I am at your son's lack of progress.'

'N-no, ma'am,' stuttered Dad. 'But if you want to, f-feel free. I do love the sound of your v-voice.'

'QUIET!' Demento barked.

'Yes, ma'am.'

'Danny Dread has thus far shown a complete lack of ability in the ways of evil. More worrying still, he has demonstrated zero desire to improve,' she said. 'Even though he did club Rufus Exploso on the head today, it was too little, too late.'

'You clubbed Exploso?' said Dad. 'Good work.'

Dame Demento clutched Dad's face in one hand, smushing his cheeks and making him look like a goldfish.

'If the boy does not improve next term, I will throw him out of the Academy. Am I making myself clear, Mr Dread?'

'Mmm hmm, yss mmm, vry clr.'

'Good,' she said, and then stalked away to terrify someone else.

'Demento can't kick you out,' said Dad, suddenly feeling braver once she was out of earshot. 'The Dreads make this place what it is. My father is the head of the board!'

'He's the head, all right,' Danny mumbled.

'What?'

'Nothing,' said Danny. 'But, I don't know . . . maybe I'm just not evil enough?'

Dad Dread grabbed his chest as if he'd been shot. 'Don't be ridiculous, my boy. You're a late bloomer, that's all. We Dreads have been evil geniuses since time immemorial. Just because things aren't going great right now doesn't mean they never will. We're only one evil idea away from immortality. Plus, if you don't stick at it, who else will continue our illustrious heritage?'

'Well, you're not doing such a great job yourself.' A familiar voice cut through Dad's rant.

They turned around and, standing before them, like a pair of tiny gargoyles, were Rufus Exploso and his father, Dr Ralfus Exploso. Rufus had a bandage around his head.

'Oh, it's you, Exploso,' said Dad. 'Haven't you retired yet?'

Exploso Senior smirked. 'I'm not the one being told off by Dame Demento in the corridor. Seems you're as useless now as you were when we were kids.'

'Oh, yeah?' said Dad. 'Well, at least I've grown since then.'

Exploso grunted and clenched his fists. His aggression made up for his lack of physical presence—a bit like a black widow spider or a Yorkshire terrier.

'Face it, Dread,' he said. 'You're useless. You've never come up with a decent scheme and you never will.'

Dad chuckled and casually checked his fingernails. 'Well, shows what you know, Exploso,' he said. 'Because I have just hatched the most sinister, most dastardly, most diabolical plan the world has ever seen. Once it's complete, you might as well quit, because there is no way you will ever top it.'

Danny rubbed his eyes. This happened every Parents' Evening.

'What is it, Dread?' said Dirk Trenchfoot, who'd stopped next to the Explosos.

'Yes, tell us,' said Hector Blackheart, who'd joined in the scrum with a gang of other parents. 'What is so good that it's going to put us all to shame?'

They all stared at the Dreads. Danny wanted to disappear. His dad shutting up would have been good, too. No such luck.

'Fine,' said Dad to the assembled crowd. 'If you're so desperate to know how brilliant I am, I'll tell you. I have hatched a plan . . . to control all of the world's . . . sharks!'

There was silence.

'Then what?' said Exploso.

'What do you mean?' said Dad.

'Once you've controlled all the sharks in the world— then what will you do?'

Dad smirked to himself.

BRAINWASHED SHARK

'Well, if you must have EVERYTHING explained to you like some sort of IDIOT, I'll tell you. I will coerce the sharks into eating all the fish,' he said. 'And do you know what will happen then?'

'You'll have very fat sharks?' said Hector Blackheart.

'No, you fool,' said Dad. 'People will be starving, and begging me to let them catch fish again. They will pay any amount to get me to call off the feeding frenzy.'

'So you're going to threaten people with fish?' said Exploso. 'Great plan, Dread.'

'I know,' said Dad, who didn't really get sarcasm. 'Now, if you'll excuse me, we'll be going. Evil isn't going to do itself!'

As they walked away, Danny heard them sniggering.

Dad Dread strode down the long, stone staircase towards the aircraft park. Danny struggled to keep up,

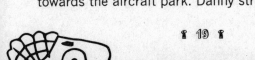

pulling his heavy suitcase behind him.

'Doesn't that bother you?' said Danny.

'What, son?'

'You know, Exploso making fun of you.'

Dad tittered to himself and shook his head. 'The thing you need to learn about Ralfus Exploso,' he said, 'is that Ralfus Exploso is an idiot. He was an idiot when we were kids and he's an idiot now.'

Danny tried not to lose his case down one of the huge potholes. 'He has done quite a few schemes lately, though.'

Dad tensed up but tried not to let it show. 'Of course he has,' he said. 'But Exploso has it all wrong. He goes for quantity over quality.'

Danny nodded as if he understood what Dad was going on about.

'You see, son,' Dad continued, 'Exploso thinks he's a big shot, just because he hacked into the stock market and stole all the money. Well, do you know something? I could have done that.'

'Really?' said Danny, trying not to sound too disbelieving.

'Yes, really,' said Dad. 'But do you know why I didn't? Because it's too easy. I am an artist, not a hack. When I hatch a plan, it has to be completely original.'

Danny nodded glumly. He'd already heard this speech a gazillion times before. They carried on walking, past all the giant angels of destruction that slumbered on the tarmac, all sleek and black and deadly.

'So don't worry, my boy. One day he will learn that we Dreads are just as good—no, scratch that—BETTER than him and all his lousy hangers-on,' said Dad.

'Where's our plane?' said Danny.

Dad stopped and rubbed his forehead. 'It's, um, in the garage for repairs,' he said. 'I've had to borrow one.'

He nodded at an ominous black and chrome aircraft at the end of a row. It had a huge pointed nose and immense rockets mounted under the wings.

'Wow,' said Danny. 'That's actually better than our normal ship.'

'No, not that one,' said Dad, then pointed at something behind it. 'That one.'

Danny was shocked when he realized the thing he was pointing at was actually an aircraft. It was made entirely of wood, with canvas wings, a bit like sails on a pirate ship. It was sixteen times smaller than all the other craft and had just enough room inside for Dad, Danny, and one suitcase.

'How is it powered?' said Danny.

'Pedal,' said Dad.

'But that'll take—'

'Seventeen hours,' said Dad. 'Hope you're feeling energetic, son.'

Chapter Four

They'd been flying for three hours and had only travelled ninety miles. The pedals made the canvas wings flap up and down like a bird's. Danny's legs burned. It didn't help constantly being overtaken by other aircraft. The turbulence in their wake was so bad it almost made him lose his lunch.

'So,' said Dad, trying to get some kind of conversation going, 'have you seen much of your grandfather at school?'

'Not really,' said Danny, being careful not to admit that he'd been avoiding him. 'Except today.'

'What happened today?'

Danny thought about it. He could either lie and tell him that Granddad Dread had said something nice to him, or he could tell the truth. He thought that if Dad knew about Granddad's dim view of his evil abilities he might take Danny out of the Academy. Here goes nothing.

'He told me I'm a disgrace to the family name,' said Danny.

'Hmm, yes, he used to say that to me,' said Dad.

'Why do you think I had his head shipped to the school? Why did he say that, anyway?'

Danny pedalled harder. 'Because he heard Rufus Exploso giving me a hard time about something that happened in class.'

A grim look fell over Dad Dread's face. Danny's heart jumped. It's happening, he thought. Dad is finally admitting to himself that I'm no good as an evil genius.

'That's it!' Dad yelled.

Yaaaaaay! I'm out!

'It's one thing to be mocked by my peers—I can take that, they're all morons anyway—but it's quite another when my father turns on his own flesh and blood. Especially when you were up against an Exploso!' Dad pumped the pedals, a snarl plastered across his face.

'This has gone too far!' he cried. 'We are going to show them!'

Oh no.

'Yes, we're going to show all of them—Exploso, Trenchfoot, Blackheart, Demento, and now Phileas Dread. They are going to see that we Dreads are the evillest, sickest, most maniacal villains this world, nay, this UNIVERSE has ever seen!'

'But Dad . . .' said Danny.

'Not now, son.' Dad silenced him with a raised hand. 'With the dark demons of Hell as my witness, I am going to execute the most dastardly plan ever conceived, and you, my boy, are going to help me. Then, when the dust has settled and we RULE this stinking planet, we will walk into that school at the end of the summer with our heads held high and we will say, "WHO'S LAUGHING NOW?"'

Dad cackled like a hyena on helium and wouldn't stop until a pelican flew into one of the wings, nearly causing them to crash.

Chapter Five

By the time the Dreads' pedal-powered plane staggered into the lair, Danny was ready to collapse. The pelican incident had added an extra two hours to the journey. He fell straight into bed and didn't stir for the next twelve hours.

Danny was awoken by a nudge on his hand. He blearily opened his eyes, expecting to see Dad, but he wasn't there. In fact, no one was there. Well, no human anyway.

'Ugh, a rat!'

Danny leapt out of bed and stared at the little grey creature sitting on his bed. Dad always had rats in the lab for experiments, but they never normally woke Danny up. And they never normally had human ears growing out of their backs.

Danny crouched down to get a closer look. If he didn't know better, he'd say the rat was smiling.

TALKING RAT!

'You're a strange-looking thing, aren't you?' said Danny.

'Well, I don't see your face winning any prizes.'

Danny screamed and jumped back up.

'You can talk?'

'SO CAN YOU!' the rat yelled.

'But . . . how?'

'I'm special,' said the rat. 'Me and a few of my brothers and sisters were rounded up by your dad and had his cloned parts grown on our backs. He said they would be handy replacements if he ever blew any of his bits off in an explosion.'

'So there are more of you?' said Danny, amazed.

'Yeah, but I'm the only one who can talk,' the rat said with a proud grin. 'When your dad was splicing my genes, he must have accidentally given me the ability to speak or something. OH MY GOD, CAN WE BE FRIENDS?'

'Um . . .' Danny blinked hard. This wasn't the easiest thing to wake up to. 'I suppose so?'

'AMAZING!' he yelled. 'It's been so lonely around here having no one to talk to. I mean, I used to be really close to my brother, but he can't talk human so it's not the same. Plus, your dad grew a foot on his back and now he can't figure out which way up to run. HA HA HAAA!'

Headache storm clouds began to gather behind Danny's eyes. 'Why couldn't you talk to my dad?'

'I tried, but he said he must have been imagining it and that if he had a talking rat, he would have to do loads of experiments on him. And can I tell you a secret?'

He gestured for Danny to come closer. Danny did so.

'I DON'T LIKE EXPERIMENTS!' the rat shouted.

Danny's ears rang. 'So, do you have a name?'

'Well, the cloning experiment was called Electronic Amendment of Rats in Laboratories, so call me Earl!' said the rat, that grin still plastered across his face.

'Yeah, hi Earl, I'm Danny.'

Earl reached out, grabbed Danny's finger with his tiny paw and shook it. 'Pleased to meet you. But I know who you are—your dad is always going on about you. "My Danny will be the next great super-villain" this, and "Danny will be the scourge of all things good" that.' He stopped and squinted at the gawky-looking human. 'Are you really that evil?'

'NO!' Danny blurted. 'I mean YES. Of course I am. The evillest.'

'I knew it!' said Earl. 'I could tell just by looking at your face. You're not evil.'

Danny didn't know what to say.

'It's OK, Danny,' said Earl. 'I am the best at keeping secrets. My brother Steve told me a secret once and I've kept it to myself for AGES. Want to know what it is?'

'Um, OK.'

'WELL, I'M NOT TELLING!' Earl yelled. 'See? I am the top secret-keeper in the world.'

Danny narrowed his eyes and cocked his head. For a rat, Earl seemed trustworthy.

'Fine,' said Danny. 'To be honest, Earl, I'm just not that good at being evil.'

'I KNEW it!' Earl clapped his front paws together. 'Don't worry, though. My lips are zipped!'

Danny smiled. It felt good to open up to another person. Well, not person, but close enough.

'Hey, shall we go and see your dad?' said Earl. 'He hasn't been to bed since you got back. I think he needs cocoa or something.'

'You're joking,' said Danny.

Earl shook his head. 'Nope. He's been in his lab the whole time, shouting about someone called Exploso. I think that shark scheme not working upset him.'

'Oh, so he's already done it?' said Danny. 'The way he was talking at the Academy, it sounded like it was still ongoing.'

'I doubt it,' said Earl. 'A couple of weeks ago, he tried to brainwash a load of sharks. Problem was, their brains were so TINY that they eventually forgot that they were being controlled. And that's when they started to get bitey.'

'Ah,' said Danny. 'So what's he doing now?'

'I don't know,' said Earl. 'I had to leave—all the noise was hurting my ear. Before I went, he was trying to figure out how many helium balloons it would take to steal the Eiffel Tower. HA HA HAAAA!'

Danny sighed. 'Yeah, I'd better go and have a word.'

Chapter Six

The Dread lair was built into the side of a mountain. It wasn't the most state-of-the-art compound in the world, but still had all you needed for a basic super-villain set-up—aircraft launch bay, laboratory, transmission room with a giant screen and camera for making threatening videos, that kind of thing.

It had been just the two of them for as long as Danny could remember. His mum had died trying to blow another hole in the ozone layer when he was a baby, so he couldn't remember her. Thinking about how life would have been different if she were still around made Danny feel sad, but it wasn't as if he missed her. Dad didn't even keep any old photos around the lair.

Danny threw on some clothes and clomped down the grand, stone staircase.

Dad Dread's lab was cluttered and dusty and smelled like mouldy compost. Fluorescent liquids bubbled in beakers which lined every surface. The air vibrated to the hum of electrodes.

Dad stood behind his cluttered desk, dialling the Dreadphone. He hopped from foot to foot, with bags the size of hammocks hanging beneath his eyes.

'What are you doing, Dad?'

'Starting World War Three!' Dad whispered. 'Now, shhhh.'

Danny chuckled to himself and sat down in a swivel chair with Earl in his pocket. He wasn't too worried about this one.

''Ello,' Dad said in the worst French accent ever heard by human ears. 'Is zis ze White 'Ouse?'

Danny spun around in his chair and looked up, watching the cave ceiling twirl.

'Could I speak to ze prrresident of ze United States? Zis is ze prrresident of Frrrrance.' Dad winked at Danny and grinned. 'OK, well zen can you take a messaaarge? Tell 'im . . . 'e stink!'

Dad slammed the phone down and cackled. 'Now we play the waiting game!'

Since his latest humiliation at Demento's, it seemed Dad Dread had once again spiralled into a mania of plotting and planning, his head whirling with evil schemes. He was pleased that Danny was finally home. He thought a fresh mind was what was needed to come up with something spectacularly diabolical. He was about to be disappointed.

'What do you mean, you have no ideas?' he said. 'What do they teach you at that school, anyway?'

Danny couldn't think of anything to say. He loved his dad, but he was kind of full-on.

'OK,' said Dad with an exhausted sigh. 'Let's watch a little TV, see if that will help.'

Danny blew out through his lips. Most kids love TV, but not him. Not when the lair only had one channel: World News.

He followed Dad into the transmission room and sat down. Dad pressed a button on the control panel which made huge metal shutters pull back and reveal a cinema screen. He pressed another button and it flickered into life, showing the same old news channel Danny had watched billions of times before.

'When America fires the first bombs at France, we will hear about it here first,' said Dad, plonking himself down in the imposing Dread Throne. That seat had been in the family for generations. Legend had it that it was carved from the very brimstones of Hell. Or limestones from Hull—the translations are dodgy.

'And in other news,' said the anchor, Jed Blatsky, 'the Exploso family of super-villains have been foiled in their efforts to steal America's gold reserves.'

'HA!' Dad flew out of his seat and cranked up the volume to teeth-chattering levels.

'The daring heist was stopped by the Lionheart

family of superheroes, once again proving to be the finest upholders of goodness in the world.'

Danny leaned forward and watched, as footage of Ralfus and Rufus Exploso trying to blast their way into the gold bank played on the screen. What happened next made his heart gallop.

The Lionheart family flew down in their matching blue suits. First, the father, Mr Lionheart, blocked their route. When the Explosos fired at him with their ray guns, he activated his force-field, which not only protected him, but bounced the rays back at the Exploso family. Then, Mrs Lionheart used her electromagnetic disruptor powers to completely shut down their guns, and finally, their daughter, Crystallina Lionheart, froze the Explosos to the spot with her cryogenic shades.

Danny was awestruck. Dad was thrilled, too, but for different reasons.

'What did I tell you?' he screeched. 'Exploso is the most overrated super-villain since Ivan the Awkward! Always trying the most OBVIOUS plans. It's no wonder those idiotic Lionhearts were one step ahead of him.'

Dad jumped up and started pacing. 'My scheme is going to be so good—so ingenious, that there is no way the Lionhearts will be able to stop me. Then, I will thumb my nose at Exploso and say, "NEHHHH, I beat the superheroes and YOU didn't. HOW DOES IT FEEL?!"'

Danny nodded, but he wasn't really listening. He was too busy thinking about Crystallina. She was so cool, and about the same age as Danny, too. Her black hair was always tied up in a high ponytail and she had a rainbow of freckles across her nose and cheeks.

Danny had often fantasized about Mynah Boy becoming her crime-fighting partner. Not that he would ever have the guts to try anything like that for real.

With Dad Dread still ranting, Danny got out of his chair and headed for the exit.

'Where are you going, son?' Dad called after him. 'To concoct some Lionheart-busting schemes?'

'Something like that,' said Danny. 'I'll let you know if I think of anything.'

Danny and Earl went outside for some fresh air, then headed back to Danny's room and flopped down on the bed. From the bangs and explosions coming from the lab, Danny knew Dad wasn't about to walk in, so he took out his top-secret book. He hugged it to his chest, so grateful that Rufus hadn't got to see what was inside.

Danny lay the book down on the bed and carefully opened it. The drawings of Mynah Boy were at the back, but the stuff that really thrilled Danny was at the front.

Every page was crammed with news clippings about the Lionhearts. Especially about Crystallina. There were pictures of her vanquishing evil again and again. With villain after villain brought to justice. And countless innocent civilians saved from disasters. Danny tried to picture a time when those headlines might be about him.

MYNAH BOY SAVES THE WORLD.

THE PELICAN BRIEF

The pelican didn't know what had hit her.

One minute she was flying along, minding her own business, scoping out the sea for tasty fish, and the next, she was stuck in a giant wing, being dragged in the opposite direction.

The next thing she knew, she was on the side of a mountain miles away from home. In fact, she couldn't even remember where home was.

She spotted movement further down the mountain. The boy that had hit her with the wing was there. And he had something with him. It was small and grey like a rat, but it had a human ear on its back.

The pelican clacked her bill, making the air sac underneath wobble like a deflated balloon. That little rat looked delicious. She didn't normally go for rodents, but this one was something special.

She decided to attack while he was out in the open. Whenever she caught a fish, she would dive down to the ocean, scoop it out, and then swoop into the air. Surely catching a rat couldn't be that different.

She hopped off her perch and dived down at a fantastic speed, her sharp yellow beak sticking out in front of her.

Just before she could make the grab, the rat moved. Her beak stuck into the ground and her whole body vibrated like a giant arrow.

By the time she got unstuck, the rat had gone back indoors. Maybe this wasn't going to be so easy.

Chapter Seven

'You LIKE her.' Earl climbed on to Danny's shoulder and peered at the book.

'No, I don't,' said Danny, all the blood rushing to his face. 'I just think Crystallina's cool, that's all.'

'I can see why,' said Earl. 'She froze those two guys like a couple of old fish fingers. ZAP!'

'I don't know, Earl,' said Danny. 'I suppose I'm just a little jealous of her. It must be great to be able to save the world all the time.'

He flipped to the back of the book and let Earl see his Mynah Boy comic strips.

'I knew it!' Earl beamed. 'You're a superhero trapped inside the body of a super-villain! This is AMAZING!'

'Keep your voice down!' Danny panicked. That was the last thing his dad needed to hear.

Earl nodded and stage-whispered, 'SORRY.'

Danny traced a finger down a line drawing of his Mynahcraft. He had no idea how to build his own plane and had failed the module that was supposed to teach him.

'Why don't you do it?' said Earl.

Danny frowned. 'What do you mean?'

'Just go out and do it,' said Earl. 'Be Mynah Boy.'

Danny shook his head. 'It's not that easy.'

'WHY NOT?' said Earl. 'What's the worst that could happen?'

'We could be caught; we could make things worse; we could DIE.' Danny counted them off on his fingers.

Earl waved away these objections. 'Ah, you could die falling down the stairs. At least you'd be doing something you actually enjoyed. When was the last time that happened?'

Danny sighed and looked at Earl. This rat was both the stupidest and the wisest soul he had ever met.

Earl hopped up and down. 'COME ON! I could even be your trusty sidekick—Rat . . . Rat. I could just be called Rat. We would stop SO MUCH CRIME!'

A tiny flame of excitement briefly burned in Danny's chest before being extinguished under a wave of realism. 'But how could we do that? I don't even have a costume—plus, the only craft we've got is that pathetic wooden thing with a pelican-shaped hole in it.'

Earl tapped Danny's neck. 'A couple of months ago, I was living in a nest with my three hundred brothers and sisters. Now, I'm sitting here, with a big human ear on my back, talking to you as if it's the most normal thing in the world. Anything is possible.'

Danny looked at Earl, then back at his drawings. Maybe the crazy rat had a point.

Chapter Eight

The next day, Danny was doodling a new comic when the intercom in the bedroom crackled into life:

'DANNY, COME DOWN TO THE LAB. I'VE GOT A SURPRISE FOR YOU!'

For any other kid, this might have been a new bike, or a trip to Disneyland. Danny knew that it wasn't going to be anything like that, though. Unless Dad was planning to kidnap Donald Duck. Again. Earl hopped back into his pocket and they made their way down.

'Son!' Dad yelled. 'You're here just in time. Please help me welcome to the Dread Lair my new assistant— Malevolo!'

Danny looked at the creature standing in front of him. His body was withered and hunched and looked as if it could barely support his enormous, hairless, watermelon head. His tiny, piggy eyes were blown up to gigantic proportions by re-entry shield glasses, and his fingernails looked as though they hadn't been cleaned in decades.

'Um, hello?' said Danny.

'Massssster,' Malevolo hissed at Dad Dread. 'Who is thissssss?'

'This is my son, Danny,' said Dad. 'He's home from school for the summer to help me orchestrate my latest scheme.'

'But *I* am your assisssstant, Massssster,' said Malevolo.

'Well, my scheme is going to be so spectacular that it will need as many people as possible,' said Dad.

Malevolo sneered. His teeth were an unholy mixture of yellow, green, and brown.

'What happened to the other one?' said Danny. He hated Dad's last assistant, Kurrkus, and was glad to see he wasn't there when he got home. He just hoped the new one was a bit less weird. Looking at him, it seemed unlikely.

Dad's eyebrows shot up. 'E-excuse me?'

'What happened to your last assistant?' said Danny.

Dad eyeballed Danny as if to say, 'Shut up.' 'He, um, left the Dread organisation last month.'

Danny looked confused. 'But you said no one ever leaves the Dreads.'

Dad grumbled and picked at the lapel of his jacket. 'OK, fine,' he said. 'Kurrkus had an accident.'

'What kind of accident, Massssster?' said Malevolo.

'Yeah, tell us, Dad, we really want to know.'

'All right, all right!' Dad yelled. 'Kurrkus was eaten.
By a shark.'

Danny tried not to giggle, but Kurrkus had been so
horrible, it was hard not to. His idea of a good time was
chucking kittens at trains.

'That's OK, Masssster,' said Malevolo. 'I would
happily be eaten by a shark . . . for you.'

Danny could already tell he wasn't going to like this
one.

PELICAN? PELICAN'T

The pelican kept a constant watch over the entrance
to the lair. She had never wanted anything like she
wanted that rat. Sure, the mountains were by the sea,
which provided a good supply of fish, but fish weren't
exciting. Fish weren't furry and fat, with ears where they
shouldn't have ears.

The pelican was drifting off to sleep when she spotted
it. It was dark but she was sure it was the rat. Suddenly,
she felt wide awake. She swooped down to the entrance
of the lair and scooped the rat into her mouth.

It was then she realized it wasn't a rat at all. It was a
porcupine.

Chapter Nine

Malevolo soon fitted into life at the Dread lair, following Dad around like pestilence follows plague. And, far from being annoyed by it, Dad loved it. Malevolo acted more like a devoted dog than an assistant, always curious as to how to become more diabolical.

Dad's voice could be heard ringing through the lair at all hours of the day, lecturing his adoring assistant on the ways of evil.

He took Malevolo into the main lab and swept his arm around grandly, as if he were giving a tour of a country manor.

'This lair,' he boomed, 'is the result of generation after generation of evil and innovation. Every blast ray gun, every destructor beam, every exploding cupcake is the culmination of the blood, sweat, and tears of my forefathers.'

Danny lay on his bed and wrapped his pillow around his head. He had heard this speech squillions of times and could recite it in his sleep.

Malevolo, though, was entranced. His milky eyes gazed around the lair in wonder. When he saw the control panel, he licked his lips, like a normal man would when presented with a fine steak.

'Tell me, Masssster,' he said, drooling. 'Who will take on this wonderful lair when you have passed?' He stopped and wiped his wet mouth. 'Not that I wish that to happen for a verrrry, verrrrrry long time.'

Dad adjusted his goggles and smiled. 'Why, Danny, of course. He is the one true heir to the lair.'

Malevolo's face screwed up. 'Hmm. Yessss.'

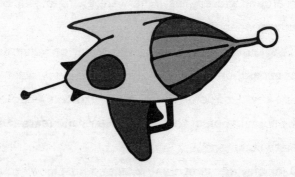

Chapter Ten

'Hey, Danny, what do you think of this?' said Earl.

Danny got up and went over to the rug in front of the wardrobe. Earl had stuck a pen in his mouth and drawn an M on an old yellow jumper.

'It's all right,' said Danny. 'But I need a bit more than that.'

'Like what?'

'Well, a cape would be nice.'

Danny still wasn't sure about this whole superhero thing. It was a nice thing to dream about, but to actually do it was something entirely different. His dad would be heartbroken if he found out and he wasn't sure he wanted to risk it.

Earl frowned and stroked his chin. Then his face lit up. 'I've got just the thing!' He scurried through a hole in the wall and reappeared a minute later with a bin liner. 'Ta da!'

'Actually, I can probably do without one.'

Earl shrugged. 'Are you sure? 'Cos if it's a quiet crime day, you can use it to pick up litter!'

Danny gave Earl a non-committal smile.

'So we're ready to go then?' said Earl. 'This is SO EXCITING!'

'NO!' said Danny. 'We can't do it yet because . . . ah . . . I need a mask.'

Earl looked Danny's face up and down. 'Don't be so hard on yourself, I'm sure you'll grow into your looks.'

Danny raised his eyebrows, unamused.

Earl giggled to himself as he scurried into Danny's still unpacked suitcase. 'Wow, it stinks in here. Do you go to the Academy of Evil Smells or what? HA! I just did a JOKE!' He stopped for a second. 'Ooh, I've found something.'

He emerged from the bag carrying a balaclava. It was part of Danny's Diamond Heist class uniform. He dropped it at the head of the jumper, then climbed on to the windowsill and brought down two feathers that had dropped off that weird bird he'd seen hanging around the lair. He stuck them into the top of the balaclava to give the costume a birdy sort of flavour.

'What are you waiting for? Try it on.'

Danny looked at Earl, standing on his back legs with a buck-toothed grin on his face. He couldn't refuse.

'I look like the world's most pathetic bank robber,' he said at his reflection.

'Oh no, you don't.' Earl scurried up Danny's leg and took his familiar perch on his shoulder. 'You look like . . . MYNAH BOY!'

Danny smiled. It was like seeing one of his dreams become a reality.

Chapter Eleven

Danny really didn't like Malevolo. Everything about him was creepy—the way he talked, the way his twisted, sharp-toothed smile made him look like a piranha. Every night at the dinner table, Malevolo would eat an entire skinned weasel without using cutlery. Or his hands.

For this reason, Danny was happy that over the next few days, Malevolo shut himself away in the launch area, with only the sound of explosions and maniacal laughter leaking out. If Dad's other assistants were anything to go by, whatever he was working on was bound to be a disaster.

Even with Earl around, Danny soon got bored. He logged on to the super-villain social networking site, Debasedbook and sighed. No new Fiend Requests. As it was, he only had three. And one of them was his dad.

MATT MAYHEM: Starving. The giant fly just dissolved my dinner.

(3 super-villains cackled at this)

MURRAY MAYHEM: Moustache looking pretty good. Selfie

coming up later.

(Murray Mayhem cackled at this)

LARRY DREAD: My new assistant is settling in wonderfully. Can't understand why he had no references.

HECTOR BLACKHEART: Probably because anyone incompetent enough to work with you would have none.

(27 super-villains cackled at this)

LARRY DREAD: Yeah, well . . . you stink.

Eventually, Earl persuaded Danny to venture down to the old launching bay outside the lair. The pedal-powered plane looked even more pathetic than before. Large pieces of it seemed to be rotting away and nearly every inch was splattered with seagull poo. Plus there was a hole in the wing the exact shape of a pelican.

'It's a fixer-upper,' said Earl.

'It's a wreck,' said Danny. 'There's no way we'll get anywhere in that.'

Earl stood up on his back legs and rubbed his chin the way he always did when he was pondering something. 'Well, it might not be the quickest, but we can TOTALLY fix that hole.' He nodded at a roll of canvas propped up against the wall. 'Then, once we've done that, we can go crime-busting. Where's the nearest city?'

Danny winced. 'Probably the Isle of Sheep. It's not really a city and not a lot of crime goes on there. But it has people. A few people.'

'Then that's PERFECT,' said Earl. 'Start slow, build up your rep as a superhero.'

'But,' Danny rubbed his eyes, 'what if my dad finds out?'

'He won't,' said Earl. 'We'll go out at night. He'll be tucked up in bed dreaming about bombs and explosions and crazy stuff like that.'

Danny looked at Earl's tiny face. 'Why are you so bothered?'

Earl tried to look coy. 'No reason. I just want you to be happy, Danny.'

Danny folded his arms.

'OK, OK,' said Earl. 'I do have my own reasons.' He stopped and sighed, a big, dopey smile on his face. 'I've heard talk of a magical land—they call it Rat Heaven. It's a place where rubbish and waste are piled as high as skyscrapers. A place where no banana skin is too black, no chicken leg too chewed, no mayonnaise too mouldy. A place where a rat's scavenging is never done. And—to top it all off—every day, these big machines just bring MORE!'

He sank down to the floor and propped his head up in his hands. 'I would love to visit Rat Heaven,' he said, wistfully. 'But the older I get, the more I think it doesn't really exist.'

Danny frowned. 'That's a tip. The thing you're thinking of is a tip.'

Earl shot back up, his eyes like flying saucers.

'You mean it's REAL?'

'Yeah, there's loads of them.'

'The prophecy was true,' Earl whispered. He tugged on Danny's trouser leg. 'Could we go, Danny? You know, after we've busted a few baddies?'

Danny eyeballed the tired old wooden craft. The idea of busting baddies for real made his stomach churn. 'I don't know, Earl. Maybe I'm not cut out to be a superhero.'

Earl patted Danny on the shin. 'You never know until you try, Danny. Besides, no offence, but you're not really cut out to be a super-villain, either.'

Danny thought about school and home and how he didn't fit in at either place.

'Fine,' he said. 'Let's give it a go.'

'YESSSS! RAT HEAVEN HERE I COME!'

Chapter Twelve

'Why aren't you in your costume?' said Earl. He had just done a last-minute check to make sure that Dad and Malevolo were sound asleep and had come back to the launching area to meet Danny. They had sneakily repaired the aircraft's wing earlier and, despite looking like a pile of kindling, it was ready to fly.

'It's in here.' Danny held up a plastic bag.

'OK, we need to make you a special case for that,' said Earl.

Danny's heart kung-fu-kicked his ribcage as they climbed into the cockpit. He was terrified of being caught, of embarrassing his father, and of crashing that pathetic aircraft into the sea.

He took a deep breath and pumped the pedals. It was even harder-going off the launch pad without Dad helping. The plane groaned as it lifted out of the launch pad slower than a fat seagull with arthritis.

Earl took a deep breath and whisper-shouted, 'LET'S GOOOOOOOOOOOOO—'

One hour later...

'—OOOOOOOOOOOOOOOOOOOOOOOOOO.'

'We're here—you can stop now,' said Danny.

Danny plonked the craft down on the Isle of Sheep. His legs were killing him.

'Great,' said Earl. 'Let's fight some CRIME!'

He climbed out of the craft and waited. Danny emerged a couple of minutes later in his costume. It wasn't quite the awesome introduction to the world of superheroism he had imagined.

'I feel stupid,' said Mynah Boy.

'Are you kidding? You look AMAZING,' said Earl. 'Plus, it's the middle of the night and we're standing in a field. NO ONE CAN SEE YOU! Except those sheep. HI GUYS!'

Danny shivered as a cold wind blew across the plain. He was glad of the balaclava. He stepped forward and felt something soft squelch under his foot. It stank.

'Well, this is an excellent start,' he said.

Earl hopped up on to his shoulder and they headed over the field into the town.

After walking around for half an hour they found no crimes whatsoever. A milkman accidentally dropped a bottle, but he swept it up straight away.

Still, Earl was enchanted. 'This is AMAZING,' he said. 'But it's quiet, isn't it, Danny? Don't you think it's QUIET?'

'What did you expect?' said Danny. 'It's the Isle of Sheep.'

'Hold on.' Earl tapped Danny on the ear and nodded at an old barn up a dirt track. Light spilled out of the windows and cars were parked haphazardly outside, blocking the lane.

'Look, here's a parking violation,' said Earl.

Danny tutted. 'I'm a superhero, not a traffic warden.'

'Hey, it's a start,' said Earl. 'COME ON.'

Danny just wanted to go home, but Earl was too persistent. When they got to the cars, they heard voices inside the barn.

'So first, we steal the sheep—'

Earl gasped and nudged Danny. 'Crime in progress. OMG!'

They crept closer and peered through a gap in the door. A gang of five men sat on hay bales and watched their leader. Danny recognized him; it was Doctor Klonzaki—a super-villain with a lair in the Himalayas. Dad Dread hated Klonzaki and said that any chump could invent a robotic Yeti.

'Once we have the sheep, we will own a million tons of wool,' said Klonzaki. 'Then, we will use our army of robo-grannies to knit a giant ball, which we will roll down mountains to obliterate entire cities!'

Blood thudded in Danny's ears. This was his big chance to stop something truly evil. Before he could talk himself out of it, he kicked the barn door open.

'ARGH, MY TOE!'

He hopped up and down, clutching his boot as Klonzaki and his goons stared.

'Um, can I help you?' said Klonzaki.

'S-silence, evil-doer.' Danny stopped hopping and remembered where he was. 'I am Mynah Boy!'

Earl jumped on to Danny's shoulder. 'And I am Rat ...boy. Actually, I'm not a boy. I'm just a rat. I am ... Rat! Can I get back to you when I've thought of a better name?'

Klonzaki sneered. 'I've never heard of you. What did you say your name was? Minor Boy? As in Morris Minor?'

'No, MynAH Boy,' said Danny.

'Ah, so like a coal miner?' said one of the goons.

Danny sighed. 'No, MYNAH BOY. M-Y-N-A-H. You know, like the bird.' He pointed at the feathers which stood up on top of his head like bunny ears.

'Hey, if you're a bird, why don't you lay me an egg?' asked a massive, tattooed lackey.

Danny's face suddenly felt very hot under his balaclava. 'N-no, I'm like the mynah bird. I can imitate people.'

'So your super power is that you can do voices?' said Klonzaki.

'Um . . . yes.'

They all laughed, their cackles bouncing off the high wooden ceilings.

'Well, how about this? I'll do an impression of someone who cares,' said Klonzaki. 'Tie him up, boys.'

'What?' Danny cried. Crime fighting was much easier in comics.

He struggled, but Klonzaki's cronies were too strong.

'DON'T WORRY, MYNAH BOY—YOUR TRUSTY SIDEKICK RAT WILL SAVE YOU!' Earl yelled, before sinking his teeth into a bad guy's fingers. The baddy cried out and tried to grab him, but Earl was too quick and scurried into the hay. Furious, the lackey grabbed a pitchfork and repeatedly plunged it into the bale.

'Earl!' Danny cried out as they bound his wrists together.

'Let's take him upstairs,' said Klonzaki.

The goons laughed.

'I wish all superheroes were this wimpy,' one of them drawled.

They picked Danny up and carried him outside. The biggest henchman draped him over his shoulder and climbed up a ladder on to the roof.

The ground got further and further away and Danny started to panic.

'Let me go!' Danny yelled. 'I'm not a superhero—I'm just an idiot in a balaclava.'

Klonzaki laughed. 'Don't believe him, boys, he might just be imitating a giant wuss.'

The henchmen chuckled along with their boss as they carried him over to the edge of the roof.

'Now . . . let's find out if this bird can fly,' said Klonzaki.

'NO, DON'T DO IT!' Danny screamed.

'ONE . . .' They swung him over the edge.

'NO!'

'TWO . . .' They did it again.

'NOOOO!'

'THR—'

'Oh, pack it in, will you?'

The voice came from the other end of the roof. The mob dropped Danny with a thud, knocking all the wind out of his lungs.

Danny rolled over and gasped for air. Then he saw her. It was a girl about his age. Even though she was only lit by moonlight, she looked familiar. She had black hair tied up in a ponytail and freckles on her nose and OH MY GOD, IT CAN'T BE!

Chapter Thirteen

The goons charged at the girl. She didn't even try to dodge them, but just pulled her shades down and froze them to the spot.

'DAMN YOU, CRYSTALLINAAAAA!' Klonzaki tried to run but she froze him, too, his arm outstretched and his mouth open, mid-scream.

Danny couldn't believe it—Crystallina Lionheart, his inspiration, standing there looking right at him. She was in normal clothes but it was definitely her.

'Who are you?' she said, lifting her shades.

'Mrrrrratblatta,' was what came out of Danny's mouth.

Crystallina frowned and untied him. 'Well, Mrrrahblahblah, it's nice to meet you, but you're clearly out of your depth.'

Danny nodded as the ropes fell free. 'I'm Mynah Boy,' he murmured.

'Minor Boy?' she said. 'Like, as in, that waltz was in E minor?'

'No, no, no.' Danny sighed. 'OK, yes, that's what it is. I'm Minor Boy.'

'Are you OK?' said Crystallina.

'Y-yes,' said Danny. 'I'm just a bit w-winded, that's all.'

Crystallina helped him back down into the barn.

'Earl? Are you there?' Danny called out.

Earl jumped out of the hay bale. 'I NEARLY GOT SKEWERED!' he yelled, with a massive smile on his face. Then he saw Crystallina. 'Oh, hi! I almost didn't recognize you outside of his scrapbook!'

'What?'

'N-nothing, nothing,' Danny babbled, giving Earl a 'shut up' look.

Crystallina smiled. 'A talking rat with a human ear,' she said. 'That's not something you see every day. So what brings you two to the Isle of Sheep?'

'We're fighting crime,' said Earl, flexing his front leg like a bodybuilder.

'Well, it's obviously going really well,' said Crystallina.

'Yeah, we're, um, beginners,' said Danny. He had to remind himself to stop staring. 'So, what, uh, brings you here?'

Crystallina sat down on a bale and picked at a length of straw. 'Just passing by,' she said. 'I sometimes escape at night and see what I can find. Between you and me, it's kind of boring.'

'What is?' said Danny.

'You know?' she said. 'Being a superhero.'

Danny's jaw dropped. 'How can it be boring? Being a superhero is the best thing anyone could be.'

Crystallina blew a raspberry and clamped the straw between her teeth. 'Trust me, it isn't,' she said. 'Sometimes I think it'd be more fun being a villain.'

'NO, IT ISN'T,' Danny yelled.

Crystallina looked at him strangely.

'I mean, no, I don't imagine it is.'

She sat up and narrowed her eyes at Danny. 'Who are you, anyway?'

Danny touched his balaclava, then quickly slapped his hand back down on his thigh. 'Mynah Boy—I'm Minor Boy.'

'Wow, you're really sticking to the whole alter-ego thing, aren't you?' she said. 'Most of us aren't bothered around other superheroes. I mean, you wouldn't believe who Fireball Man really is.' She cupped a hand around her mouth and whispered, 'He's a Geography teacher.'

'Well, I'm not anything interesting,' said Danny. 'Nothing at all.'

He knew he couldn't tell her who he really was. It might have got his dad in all kinds of trouble. Plus, there was no way she would trust him if she knew his true identity.

Crystallina smiled and nodded. 'I get you,' she said.

'Well, if you ever find yourself in another situation, get in touch.' She reached into her jeans pocket and flicked something at Danny. He caught it and watched it glistening in his hands. It was a small, blue metal L-shape with a tiny button on the side.

'It's a Lionheart Communicator,' she said. 'Whenever you need me, you can use that.'

Danny could barely speak. Not only had he met Crystallina Lionheart, he now had a twenty-four-hour line to her. 'Th-thanks.'

'No worries,' she said. 'Plus, that balaclava intrigues me—I like a bit of mystery.'

Danny blushed so hard, he was sure it would be visible even through the mask.

'To be honest, Crystallina,' said Earl. 'I know what's under there, and sometimes mystery is better than reality.'

Chapter Fourteen

It was almost dawn by the time they got back to the lair, but Danny didn't want to sleep anyway. It was the danger that made it exciting—sneaking out undetected, challenging a super-villain and, above all, meeting CRYSTALLINA.

He would never have dared to do something like that if it hadn't been for Earl. Maybe Dad messing with rat genes was the best thing to ever happen to Danny.

They went to the Isle of Sheep every night after that, but it didn't quite live up to their first trip. There was no crime and, more importantly, no Crystallina. He knew he had the communicator, but he thought she might get angry with him if he called her for no reason. And the last thing he wanted to do was annoy Crystallina. She could turn him into an ice lolly.

In fact, over the course of a whole week of sneaking out, this was all Danny had to add to his crime-fighting CV:

RESCUED A CAT FROM UP A TREE. THE CAT THEN CHASED EARL BACK UP THERE.

- **RESCUED EARL FROM UP A TREE. LEFT THE CAT.**

- **MIMICKED POLICE SIRENS TO SCARE AWAY A BURGLAR.**

- **REALIZED THE BURGLAR WAS JUST A MAN IN A STRIPY JUMPER.**

- **PUT A STOP TO SHAMELESS PUBLIC NUDITY. MUCH TO THE ANNOYANCE OF THE LIFE-DRAWING CLASS.**

One night after yet another trip, Danny gave the aircraft a looking over. It surely only had a couple more journeys in it before it splintered into matchsticks.

Danny couldn't have that—the rickety old thing was Mynah Boy's only way of getting out and preventing some actual evil. He didn't consider what Dad was cooking up in the lab to be a threat—the president of the World Bank was probably too clever to slip on a banana skin.

They were sitting in Danny's room one morning trying to figure out a way to fix the plane when the door swung open and Dad ran in. He never knocked.

'Hello, son!' he yelled. 'Say, who were you talking to in here?'

'No one,' said Danny. 'Just practising my Evil Speeches homework.'

'Oh, anyway, anyway.' Dad flattened his hair only for it to spring back up like an antenna. 'Come down to the launch area. Malevolo is ready for the grand reveal.'

Danny shuddered and hoped that he was 'revealing' that he was leaving.

He followed Dad, with Earl in his pocket. He wasn't too worried—every assistant of Dad's so far had been useless and ended up expiring as part of some hare-brained scheme. Malevolo would probably be no exception.

When they got down there, he was pacing around with his hands behind his back, his grey tongue flicking out and licking his disgusting teeth.

'Massssster.' Malevolo bowed as they entered the room. 'I am so fiendishly excited for what I am about to show you.'

Behind him, an enormous machine of some kind was covered in a sheet. Danny wondered where he'd managed to get a sheet that big. It looked like Godzilla's duvet. What was underneath must have been the thing he had been working on for so long.

'What I am about to show you, O evil one, is at the very cutting edge of evil technology. No other villain in the world will have anything better. With this, you will leave them all trrrrembling in your wake, O mighty liege!'

Earl made a snoring noise and Danny spluttered with laughter.

'What was that?' Malevolo barked. 'I have excellent hearing and I heard a noise.'

'Don't know,' said Danny. 'Maybe you're going mad or something.'

Malevolo narrowed his already piggy eyes and limped over to Danny. His nose twitched like a hound stalking a rabbit. Or a rat.

'What is . . . thisss?' he hissed at Earl, whose head was poking out of Danny's pocket.

'Um, it's obviously a rat with an ear attached to its back,' said Danny contemptuously.

'Danny, don't be cheeky,' Dad warned. 'Please, Malevolo, continue.'

Malevolo stared at Earl a while longer before turning around and carrying on.

'Now, the reason I have constructed this machine is because I know your existing one is inoperable, due to shark-related damage, Massssster. But rest assured that this replacement is practically invulnerable to any kind of attack, animal or otherwise. My Massssster, Lord of Evil, Minister of Mayhem, Duke of Darkness, I give you . . .' He pulled off the sheet. ' . . . the Drrrrrreadcraft!'

It was almost as tall as the ceiling—the maximum size for the launch pad, and was completely black, with DREAD ENTERPRISES printed on the side in red. Under the wings, the most sophisticated arsenal of lethal weapons known to man glistened under the lights. Danny gulped.

'I don't know what to say, Malevolo,' said Dad, tears of demented joy brimming in his eyes. 'This is the most diabolical thing I have ever seen.'

Malevolo smiled, which had to be at least the second most diabolical thing he'd ever seen.

'What do you think, son?' said Dad, squeezing Danny's shoulders tight.

'It's . . . yeah. Good. What are you planning on doing with it?'

Dad and Malevolo exchanged a quick glance. 'Good question, son . . . Um, Malevolo?' said Dad.

Malevolo's scratched his bald head. 'Well, it is up to you, Masssster.'

Dad blinked. 'I'm, uh, sure we'll think of something. But just look at it, son. Isn't it INCREDIBLE?'

Danny didn't want to acknowledge the twinges of jealousy. He remembered when he used to draw pictures for his dad when he was younger. He would usually sketch nice things like a group of happy dogs, wagging their tails and chasing butterflies. He would bring them to Dad, working hard in the lab, and Dad would make a big show out of how much he loved them.

THE DREADCR

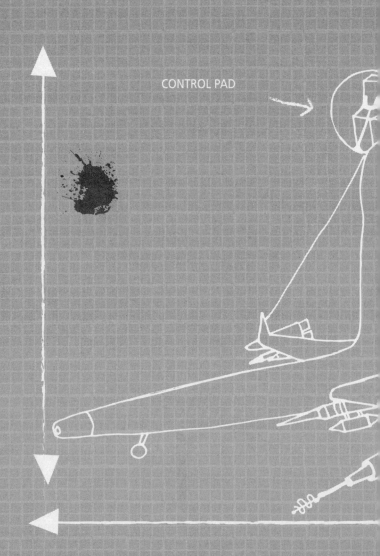

CONTROL PAD

KEY FEATURES

BLASTER RAY CANNONS

DESTRUCTO ROCKETS

HIGH-SPEED ZIP LINE

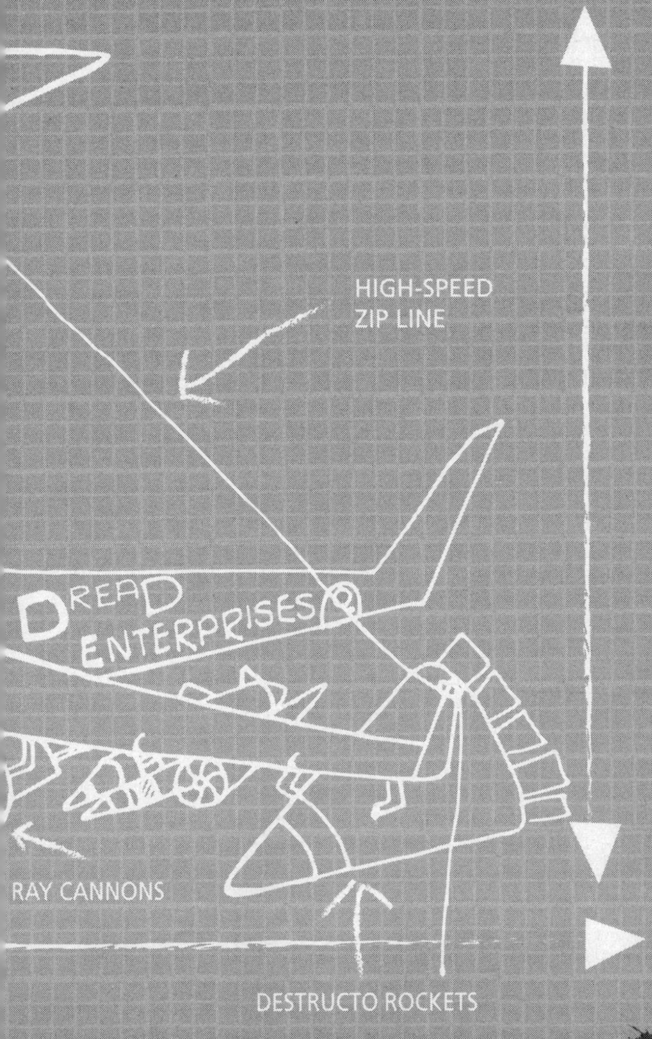

HIGH-SPEED
ZIP LINE

DREAD ENTERPRISES

RAY CANNONS

DESTRUCTO ROCKETS

'Ohhh, son, this is wonderful!' he would boom. 'A pack of snarling wolves! I'm going to put this right on my chemicals cabinet so I can look at it ALL THE TIME!'

Even though he completely misunderstood the pictures, Danny would feel so proud that his dad loved his work. Now, this giant aircraft was making his drawings look like nothing.

Before Danny could say anything, the BREAKING NEWS music boomed from the TV in the communications room. They turned and ran in, as they always did. BREAKING NEWS often meant a new disaster to take advantage of.

'All the world's leaders are meeting in London for a summit next week. Top of the agenda is world peace.'

Malevolo squinted at Dad and sneered. Sure enough, it set him off.

'Peace?' Dad spat the word out as if it was a bad crisp. 'Yuugggh! I think I'm going to be sick! Imagine a world of peace. Could you think of anything more BORING?'

'Yes, Masssster, you're so right, Masssster,' Malevolo snivelled.

'We have to find a way to use this summit to our advantage. To stop them achieving world peace and make them create world devastation.' Dad paced up and down, his hands clenching and unclenching. Then

he stopped and a devilish grin spread across his face.
'And I think the Dreadcraft will be the only thing deadly
enough to do it.'

Dad and Malevolo cackled, but Danny couldn't
join in. For the very first time, one of Dad's schemes
actually looked like it might work.

Chapter Fifteen

Danny and Earl stood outside Malevolo's room later that night. Danny knew he would be hiding the ship's blueprints somewhere in there. If he could get hold of them, maybe he could secretly disable some of the more deadly parts so nobody would get hurt at the World Peace Summit. Plus, he could also use them to create a replacement craft for the wooden one. Then, the possibilities for Mynah Boy would be endless.

Danny took out a small tube out of his pocket. He pressed a hidden button on the side and a miniscule lens popped out of the end. It was a spying device from his Evil Espionage class. All he'd used it for so far was watching out for Exploso at school, so he knew to lock his door.

Danny carefully inserted the device into the keyhole of Malevolo's door, then looked into the other end. Using tiny controls on the side, he moved the camera lens around until he could see Malevolo.

Malevolo lay asleep on his bed. Even though the walls were reinforced with titanium, they could still hear him snoring like a pig with a chest infection.

Danny zoomed in and saw the blueprints sitting on the bedside table. There was no way he'd be able to get them himself.

'You're going to have to go in,' Danny said to Earl. 'Grab the blueprints, bring them out here so I can photograph them, and then replace them without Malevolo noticing.'

Earl puffed out his chest. 'It would be an honour, Mynah Boy.'

Danny's heart thudded. This was a huge risk but world peace could be at stake.

He carefully removed the vent grill and placed Earl inside. He knew it led straight into Malevolo's room.

'Good luck.'

Earl saluted and scurried into the vent.

Danny crouched and looked through the spy device. He saw Earl scrambling out of the vent, down the shelves, and on to the floor.

Danny's stomach tingled. It was fun, all this spying stuff.

Then it stopped being fun.

Malevolo's snore caught in his throat. Panicked, Danny refocused the device. Malevolo's eyes were closed, but something wasn't right. Danny couldn't see Earl at all. There was silence. Then, Malevolo carried on snoring.

Danny took a deep breath and stepped away from the door. He was so scared that Malevolo was about to wake up and discover Earl. Danny could imagine how Malevolo would react—he'd probably scream, 'RRRRRAT!'

Wait, did that actually happen?

He looked back through the scope.

Malevolo was up and stamping at the floor.

'GET OUT, YOU INFERNAL CREATURE!'

Danny stifled a little scream. The stamping made him feel sick. When he saw Earl appear in the vent, he could have jumped for joy.

Super-quick, Earl scrabbled down the wall, across the corridor, and through a tiny hole that led to the basement.

Malevolo's door flew open. Danny dived into the utility room before he could be seen.

He watched through a crack in the door as Malevolo stalked the corridor, his nose twitching. 'I'll find you, rrrrat!' he squawked, shuffling off in search of Earl.

Like to see you try, you weirdo, Danny thought.

When Malevolo was safely around the corner, Danny jumped out and went back to the room. The door was still open. Looking around to make sure Malevolo wasn't coming back, Danny ducked inside and found the blueprints. He took his spy camera out and photographed them, making sure he got good, clear images.

Danny put the blueprints back exactly as he found them and returned to the corridor only to find Malevolo storming towards him.

'What are you doing here?' the assistant hissed. 'And where is your rrrrat?'

'Um . . . one, it's my house, and two, none of your business,' said Danny.

Malevolo rubbed his hands together. 'Something is happening here, and I intend to get to the bottom of it. I have a nose for trouble.'

'And a face for nausea,' Danny mumbled.

Malevolo grunted and pushed past Danny into his room, where he slammed the door and fastened all five of his locks.

Chapter Sixteen

Danny met up with Earl later to go over the blueprints.

'Are these useful, Danny?' said Earl. 'That crazy guy nearly stamped my tail off.'

'Definitely,' said Danny. 'There's loads to be getting on with.'

He studied the plans he had printed off, figuring out how to disable the weapons and what he would need to make his own, smaller plane. He vaguely remembered some of his Instruments of Death design class and was sure he could blag the rest.

Danny ran his finger down the images of the blueprints and tried to visualize his finished craft. He pictured himself hurtling across the sky with Crystallina and Earl, defeating the dastardly Malevolo without anyone ever discovering his true identity.

Danny's door opened. This was becoming a thing. He made a mental note to fit a lock and shoved the prints under his pillow.

'What's up?' Danny shuddered at the sight of Malevolo standing in his doorway.

'Danny.' Malevolo spat the name out as if it was

painful. 'Is it true that you sent that rrrrrat into my room to steal from me?'

'Rat? What rat?' said Danny.

'The rrrrrat with the ear on his back,' said Malevolo. 'The rrrrrat that is in your pocket.'

He pointed at Earl, who was trying to look casual, hanging out of Danny's jacket.

'That could have been any rat with an ear on him,' said Danny.

Malevolo shook his head and stepped closer. His nostrils twitched rapidly. 'This was the one.'

'Nope,' said Danny. 'You're wrong.'

'Well, if I am wrong,' said Malevolo, 'then explain this!'

He reached into his pocket and pulled out a lollipop.

'That's a lollipop,' said Danny. 'Didn't know you had a sweet tooth, Mal.'

'It's Malevolo!' he barked, spittle flying from his mouth.

Danny's eyes bulged.

'Sorry,' said Malevolo, taking a deep breath. 'I meant, explain this.'

Malevolo pulled out the spy device Danny had used on his door.

Oh, crud! He thought he'd been so careful.

'What's that?' said Danny.

Malevolo ran his tongue over his teeth. 'You know very well what this is. It's for spying! Why would you invade my privacy?'

Danny laughed. 'If I was going to spy on anyone in their bedroom, it wouldn't be you. In fact, you're the last person in the world I'd want to see in their pants.'

Malevolo growled. 'That's it! I'm going to dust this for prints. Give me a finger.'

'Don't tempt me,' said Danny.

He heard Earl chuckle softly in his pocket, which made Malevolo's ears twitch. Before he could say anything, the door flew open.

'Oh, Danny!' Dad yelled. Then his face dropped. 'Malevolo, what are you doing here?'

'Oh, nothing, Massssster,' Malevolo breathed. 'Young Danny and I were having a friendly . . . chat?'

Dad looked at them both for what felt like an age before his expression thawed into a big smile. 'Ah, it's so WONDERFUL to see the two of you getting on.'

Danny stared into Malevolo's eyes. He was slightly horrified by the way he could go minutes without blinking.

'Yes, Massssster,' said Malevolo. 'We are getting to know one another very well indeed.'

Chapter Seventeen

Even by evil-lair standards, the dinner table that night was not exactly bursting with friendliness. The only sound was Malevolo sucking bones clean and grunting.

The World Peace Summit was due to start in a couple of days and they had no real plans as to how to disrupt it. A rocket blast would only cause so much damage, and would not achieve what Dad wanted—the start of World War Three.

'If you will forgive my impetuousness,' said Malevolo, 'I have noticed that the young massssster has yet to venture an idea for our cause.' He eyeballed Danny from the other side of the table, weasel juice dribbling down his chin.

'You're right, Malevolo,' said Dad. 'Why haven't you been contributing, son?'

Danny put down his knife and fork and swallowed. He racked his brains for the lamest plan he could think of. 'All right,' he said. 'How about . . . we sneak into the world leaders' bedrooms, unplug their lamps, then leave the plugs with the pins facing up? They get out of bed—in the dark, remember 'cause no lamps—and,

OUCH! Am I right? Unless they get their slippers on first, of course.'

Dad and Malevolo stared at him.

'With respect, young Masssster, that scheme is probably not too practical.'

Dad raised a hand. 'No, no, no, it's . . . it's not that bad. It's a start. We can, you know, work with it. Sore feet can lead people to make rash decisions, like declaring war. Maybe instead of us personally unplugging things, we can persuade them to do it themselves.'

'Yep, brainwash people to step on plugs—sounds like a good plan.' Danny chuckled to himself.

No one spoke, but then Malevolo's eyes suddenly went wide, like manholes.

'I think the young masssster has given me an idea.'

Oh no.

'What is it, Malevolo?' said Dad.

Malevolo's hands shook as the diabolical scheme formed in his mind. 'You, Masssster, in your endless brilliance, have already created technology that can brainwash sharks. I suggest that it would be simple to adapt this work of genius so it is compatible with the human brain. Imagine the possibilities.'

He grinned and showed slivers of meat hung between his teeth.

'YES!' Dad Dread cried, sending half-chewed peas

flying across the table. 'Brilliant, Malevolo, brilliant! Quick, we should begin our work right away.'

They scuttled out of the dining room and down to the lab.

'So,' said Earl, nibbling at their leftovers, 'what do you think to that?'

'I think it sounds like trouble,' said Danny.

Chapter Eighteen

The lab buzzed with activity, the air thick with the sound of bubbling chemicals, heavy drills, and shrieking laughter.

'Massssster.' Malevolo called Dad Dread over to his workbench, where a beaker of purple liquid swirled and frothed above an open flame. Danny went along to watch. 'I believe I have successfully adapted the shark brainwashing formula to work on humans,' Malevolo continued, with a dastardly grin.

Dad slapped Malevolo on the shoulder. 'Brilliant! Amazing! Just think of the wickedness we could wreak with a brainwashed world leader doing our bidding.'

Danny panicked. The idea of anyone in power being under the Dread influence made his skin turn ice-cold. He had to do something.

'The fumes are getting right up my nose,' he said, making what he hoped was an accurate pantomime of someone with a cold. 'Ahh ahhh, achooooo!'

He lurched forward and flung his arms out, knocking the beaker to the floor, where it smashed into hundreds of pieces.

'Oops.'

'DANNY, WHAT HAVE YOU DONE?' Dad screeched. 'With that formula, we could have controlled a world leader and made him start a brutal war! I could have been DICTATOR OF THE WORLD!'

Danny tried to look sorry. 'I am such a klutz,' he said.

Malevolo slithered his hand along Dad's shoulder. 'Don't fear, Massssster. That wasn't the only batch.'

Dad took his head out of his hands. 'Really?'

Malevolo nodded and fixed his icy gaze on Danny. 'I would never be so careless when . . . accidents like that can happen.'

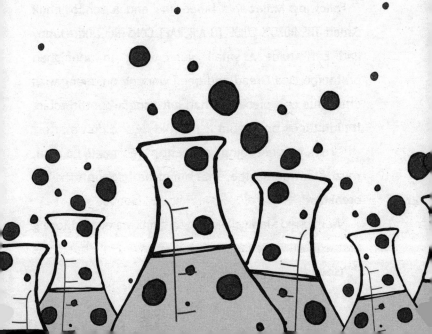

Chapter Nineteen

Later that night, Danny and Earl sneaked away from the lab and went down to the basement to get to work on their own plane. There was no way they could sabotage the Dreadcraft without the keys and they were always with Malevolo. Danny would have to fly to the Summit and warn them himself, or at least call the Lionhearts once they were at a safe distance from the lair. As much as Danny hated what Dad was planning, he couldn't give away their location.

Following Malevolo's blueprints and a school book called **THE BOZO'S GUIDE TO AIRCRAFT CONSTRUCTION**, Danny and Earl made a small plane using an unfinished prototype Dad Dread had been working on, along with other bits and pieces he had left lying around the lab. It didn't look pretty, but if it could fly, it didn't matter.

'Great, let's get going,' said Earl. 'We'll get to London, warn them about the attack and be back in time for breakfast!'

'Wait,' said Danny. 'Don't you think we should test it first with dummies or something?'

'Good thinking,' said Earl.

Danny wheeled the craft on to the mini launch pad outside and set it up. He had constructed two dummies to sit in the cockpit—one boy and one rat.

Danny stepped back to a safe distance and his heart raced. He held a unit which would control the plane once it had launched. He'd played with remote control planes before, so he guessed it would be pretty much the same.

'Here we go,' said Earl.

Danny took a deep breath. 'Launching mini craft in five . . . four . . . three . . . two . . . one . . . LIFT OFF!'

The craft whooshed off the launch pad with a loud bang. Take-off could not have gone more smoothly. Danny and Earl whooped with joy.

'We've done it!' Danny yelled.

Then the plane lost power and slammed into the mountain opposite.

The nose crumpled like an accordion and the plane plummeted back down to the lair entrance. Danny and Earl ran for cover behind a rock. The head of the crash-test dummy rolled into Danny's leg and looked up at him as if to say, 'Why?'

'I think the test was probably a good idea,' said Earl.

WHERE PELICANS DARE

The pelican sat on her perch, keeping a lookout for the rat. Her stomach groaned with anticipation.

When the rat appeared with the boy, her mouth began to water. She was about to attack but they made a really big black bird fly at her at a fantastic speed. She cawed and dived off just before it smashed into her perch.

The rat was declaring war.

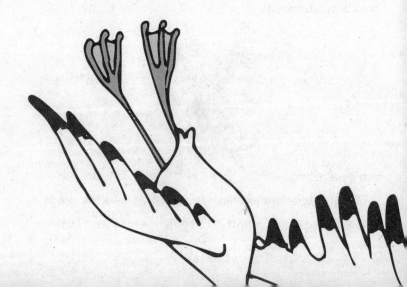

Chapter Twenty

Danny was halfway through planning another aircraft when he was called to the main lab over the intercom.

When he got there, Danny could not believe what he was seeing. How had they managed this in such a short time?

A huge steel chair stood in the corner of the lab. It had wrist and leg restraints, and a metal helmet that could be lowered down on to the head of whichever unfortunate wretch found themselves sitting in it. Glass tubes connected the helmet to two enormous cylinders filled with swirling purple gas.

'The hour has arrived, my boy,' said Dad. 'We now hold the tools to claim this world in the name of Dread.'

Oh no, Danny thought.

'Oh, brilliant,' Danny said. 'So, what do you need me for?'

'We need to test this brrrainwashing machine,' said Malevolo, rubbing his hands together. 'If it works, we can go straight to the Summit and kidnap a politician.'

Danny glared at Malevolo, then at his dad. Dad smiled nervously.

'Wait, you want to test this on *me?*'

Dad scratched the back of his head. 'Um?'

'You have got to be kidding me!'

He could see their plan now: to change him into a diabolical straight-A evil genius and dress it up so it looked like testing.

Dad shrugged apologetically. 'Sorry, I just thought you could stand to be just a little more evil,' he said. 'A smidge.'

Danny's mouth dropped open as a tide of fury threatened to pull him under. 'Fine,' he said. 'F-fine. I just need a little time to prepare.'

With that, he turned and ran out of the lab.

Chapter Twenty-One

Danny climbed into the cockpit of the wooden pirate craft and sat down heavily, making the whole thing creak. 'Let's see how much he likes Malevolo now,' he muttered.

'Where are we going?' said Earl.

Danny hadn't spoken since the brainwashing thing. He just went back to his room, threw his Mynah Boy costume, the Lionheart Communicator, and his secret book into a bag, then ran straight to the old launch area.

'We're leaving,' said Danny. 'Forever.'

Earl clasped his face between his paws.

'But what about all my brothers and sisters?' he said. 'Steve and Ernie and Percy and Sheila and Beryl and Steve II? Have you considered Steve II in all of this?'

Danny sighed. 'I'm sorry, Earl, but I have to go. I can't stay here any longer. My own dad wants to brainwash me. Wants to change who I am. If you want to stay, then fine.'

Earl got up and touched the back of Danny's hand. 'What about building a new plane and warning the Peace Summit?'

'I can't think about that now Earl. I just need to get away.'

'If this is what you really want, I'm behind you all the way. We're best friends and this is what best friends do. Plus, maybe we'll get to go to Rat Heaven after all.'

Danny took one last look at the Dread lair and wiped the tears from his eyes. He had had enough of being a let-down and a disappointment. Maybe Malevolo *was* the son Dad had always wanted. He breathed deeply and started pedalling. The craft lurched upwards into the black sky, towards the Isle of Sheep and a brand-new life.

Chapter Twenty-Two

'OK, let me try and understand,' said Earl as Mynah Boy clambered out of the groaning wooden craft. 'Our plan is to see if the Lionhearts will adopt us?'

'Pretty much,' said Danny.

'But what if they say no?'

'Then we'll just have to survive on our own in the wild,' said Danny. 'Do you know what berries are safe to eat?'

'I'm a rat; I eat them all!' said Earl. 'I am NOT fussy. Between you and me, I ate half a football this morning.'

'Fine,' said Danny.

'And I'm not even sorry.'

Danny took a deep breath. It was a still night in the field—every sheep was asleep, probably counting humans or something like that. He wondered if this was really the right thing to do. Before he could think about it too much, he pressed the button.

The communicator lit up in his hand. It crackled once, then a voice came out: 'Crystallina Lionheart?'

Danny's heart skipped several beats. 'H-hi, it's Dan-Mynah Boy. It's Mynah Boy . . . do you remember me?'

There was a pause. 'Oh, hello, Minor,' she said. 'Of course I remember you. How could I forget that fetching jumper and tea cosy combo?'

'I, um, need you to meet me at that barn on the Isle of Sheep,' said Danny. 'It's urgent.'

'Yeah, all right,' she said. 'I've got to sneak out, though. The folks don't even know I'm up. I'll see you there.'

The communicator crackled again and the lights cut out.

Danny and Earl exchanged a look. This was really happening.

The barn was empty when they arrived, but they heard voices coming from an outbuilding across the yard. Danny crept over. If a crime was in progress, foiling it would surely make the Lionhearts more likely to take them under their wing.

'Imagine it: a huge sheep AND a huge fly!' said one of the voices.

'Which one do you want to blast?' said the other.

'Why pick just one? Let's have an ARMY of giant sheep!'

Danny froze. Those voices sounded awfully familiar. Still, he had to do something.

'Stop right-a there!' He burst in and yelled in an Italian

accent. He didn't want them to recognize his voice.

'Who are you?' said Matt Mayhem.

'I am a-Mynah Boy, and I am-a here to stop you making-a big-a sheep-a.'

Murray toted his enlarger ray. 'And how are you going to do that?'

Danny scratched the back of his head. He made a mental note to come up with something to threaten baddies with. 'Um, I don't know. But Crystallina Lionheart is on-a the way.'

The Mayhems' eyes bulged. 'You idiot,' said Matt to his brother. '"Oooh, let's go to the Isle of Sheep," you said. "There'll be no superheroes there," you said.'

'How do we know he's telling the truth, though?' said Murray. 'He could just be some kind of whacko.'

Danny walked towards them. 'Please-a guys. I don't-a want you to be-a frozen.'

Murray squinted at Danny and thoughtfully stroked his pitiful moustache. 'You sound familiar.'

Danny shifted from side to side and averted his gaze. 'Do I? Don't be-a silly. You . . . idiota.'

'Yeah, he does,' said Matt. 'It's weird 'cause he's wearing a balaclava but he LOOKS familiar as well.'

Danny suddenly became very aware of his gangly limbs.

'And he can't be a proper superhero. I mean, look at

that costume. It looks like his granny knitted it,' said Murray.

'Hey!' Danny cried. 'I am a superhero! I'm-a doing the best-a I can-a!'

The twins spluttered with laughter.

'Let's find out who he is,' said Matt.

Danny started backing off when a voice from outside stopped him.

'Hello? Where are you, Minor?'

Panic electrified Danny's spine. 'Quick,' he whispered to the Mayhems. 'Hide.'

They looked confused.

'It's-a Crystallina!' he hissed.

The Mayhem twins shrieked and ran to the back of the room. Just as the door opened, they threw the enlarger ray to one side and jumped into a trough half full of disgusting swill. Danny knew they were terrified of her ever since she froze their evil granddad, Merton Mayhem, and sent him to jail.

'Oh, there you are.' Crystallina walked in, smiling. 'What's up?'

'*Buongiorno!*' Danny said. 'Nothing-a much-a. How are-a you?'

Crystallina folded her arms, her smile going from friendly to quizzical. 'Why are you talking like that?'

'Like-a what-a? This is how I-a always-a speak-a,' said

Danny, doing the crazy hand gestures and everything.

Crystallina giggled. 'Well, this is very entertaining, but surely you wanted me for something else?'

Danny sighed and shot a quick glance at the trough. How could he ask to join a family of superheroes when he was helping to protect a couple of villains? Even if they were his friends.

'Uh, sorry, I·a thought there was·a criminals·a hanging around, but it was a false·a alarm.'

Crystallina's freckles crinkled up into a frown. 'Are you sure?' she whispered. 'They're not in here hiding, are they?'

Danny shook his head, but it was too late—she had already seen the enlarger ray. She nodded at him as if to say, 'I've got you covered' and lowered her shades. Danny's panic shifted up a gear.

Crystallina crept through the room silently, checking behind farm equipment and stacks of wood. Danny watched in terror as she got ever closer to the trough.

'What's happening?' Earl whispered. 'And why are you talking like a pizza guy?'

'They're my friends,' Danny whispered. 'I can't give them up.'

Crystallina tiptoed round a pillar and examined a hay bale opposite the twins' hiding place.

'WAIT!' Danny called out.

Crystallina flipped her shades up. 'What is it, Minor?'

'I think I heard-a something upstairs, in-a the hay loft.'

Crystallina nodded and ran to the ladder.

'Come out with your hands up, punks!' she yelled. 'If you come quietly, maybe I won't HURT you as bad.'

Matt popped his head out of the trough and nodded at Murray. They climbed out and tiptoe-ran out of the barn.

'It's clear,' yelled Crystallina.

'Ah, see? It was a false-a alarm,' said Danny, his voice trembling. '*Mamma mia.*'

Crystallina flew back down and landed in front of him with her hands on her hips.

'Hey, if you can fly, why did you climb that ladder?' said Earl.

She shrugged. 'I like to do things like normal people if possible,' she said. 'It's not so great being different sometimes.'

'Hey, I'm a rat with some guy's ear on my back—I can relate,' said Earl.

Crystallina frowned at Danny. 'I don't get you, Minor.'

'What-a do you- a mean-a?' said Danny.

'Cut it out with the Italian accent,' she said.

'Sorry.'

'I just think you're keeping something from me.'

Danny looked right at her. Her eyes seemed to be burning holes in him. He wished she would put her shades down.

'Why won't you tell me who you are?' she said.

'I . . . I can't,' said Danny.

The reality of what he was planning to do came crashing down on him. Despite everything that was happening with Malevolo, he still loved his dad. The brainwashing had just made him so angry that he wasn't thinking straight. He wanted to tell Crystallina about Dad and Malevolo's plans for the summit, but how would he explain how he knew about it? It looked as though he was going to have to deal with it himself.

'Whose is this?' said Crystallina, nudging the discarded gun with her toe.

'It's mine,' said Danny. 'I use it to scare bad guys.'

Crystallina picked it up and examined it. 'Expander ray? So you deal with baddies by making them bigger? Good luck with that.'

Danny giggled nervously.

'I'm keeping an eye out for you,' said Crystallina. 'Because you're either the worst superhero in the world, or you're secretly on the other side.'

Little did she know, he was both.

Chapter Twenty-Three

Dad was standing outside the lair, wringing his hands, as Danny brought the shaky wooden craft in to land. Seeing how worried he looked hit Danny like a sonic boom of guilt.

'Danny!' Dad wrenched the cockpit door open and it came off in his hands. 'Where have you been?'

Danny sighed, his hands trembling as he climbed out. 'I just had to get out for a while.'

Dad threw the door down and grabbed his son's shoulders.

'I'm sorry, Danny,' he said. 'I shouldn't have agreed to try that machine on you.'

Danny sighed and gulped down what felt like a brick in his throat. 'Am I an embarrassment to you, Dad?'

Dad's mouth dropped open and his hair pinged up. 'Don't be ridiculous, Danny. I couldn't wish for a better son. Look, just because I like Malevolo doesn't mean you're not my number one boy!'

Danny's eyes prickled.

Dad put his arm around Danny. 'The only way you could disappoint me is if I found out you were secretly a superhero!' He threw his head back and cackled. Danny bunched the handles of his bag tightly and winced. He made a mental note to throw the Mayhems' expander ray off the side of the cliff outside as soon as he could. If Dad found that, he would want to know where he got it. Even worse, Malevolo could find it and put it to some kind of evil use.

'Don't worry,' said Dad. 'With our new technologies, it is only a matter of time before we rule this ghastly world. And you are going to help. Without being brainwashed.'

Danny screwed his eyes shut. 'Great.'

Chapter Twenty-Four

Dad led Danny back to the brainwashing machine.

'Malevolo and I have had a discussion and we've decided that it would be unfair to test the machine on you.'

Relief flooded through Danny.

'So instead,' Dad continued, 'we're going to try it on Malevolo.'

It was all Danny could do not to scream with laughter.

Malevolo tried to grin, but he was fooling no one. His eyes shot rays of pure hate at Danny.

Dad placed his hand on Malevolo's rounded shoulder. 'Don't worry,' he said. 'I'll be gentle.'

Malevolo sat in the chair, grumbling to himself. Dad fastened the arm restraints.

'Malevolo!' Dad yelled from the control panel. 'What is your least favourite food in the world?'

Malevolo growled, 'Ice crrrrream.'

The way he said it, you'd think he was talking about curried slugs.

Dad hammered commands into the system. 'Well, by the end of this, you will love ice cream more than anything.'

'I couldn't love anything more than you, Massssster,' he said.

Danny rolled his eyes. What a creep.

'Thank you, Malevolo,' said Dad. 'Now brace yourself. This might sting a little.'

Dad pulled a big lever and the chair groaned into life. The gases in the cylinders changed from purple to green to red. Sparks flew from the helmet.

'Uhhhhhhhhhh, muuuuhhhhhhhhh,' Malevolo groaned as his body convulsed.

Smoke shot out of the back of the brainwashing

device. Danny thought he was going to see Malevolo fried. As much as he hated him, he didn't want that to happen.

Dad pushed the lever back up and the machine wound down. Eventually, Malevolo stopped twitching. Dad ran to the pantry and came back with a big bowl of ice cream, covered in syrup and chocolate flakes.

He undid Malevolo's restraints and held the bowl in front of his nose. Malevolo's eyes shot open and he scooped great wads of ice cream out of the bowl with his hands and crammed them into his mouth.

'Goood,' he mumbled. 'Ice cream gooooooooood.'

Dad beamed triumphantly at Danny. 'Looks like we've got ourselves a brainwashing machine.'

Danny hoped his smile looked real enough to convince him.

THUS QUOTH THE PELICAN: 'OUCH!'

The pelican sat on her new perch. She saw the rat emerge into the sunlight. He was with the boy. The boy was carrying a big stick. He looked like he was going to throw it off the side of the mountain.

Sensing an opportunity, she swooped down at the rat. The boy saw her and cried out. He pressed something on the stick which blasted the pelican with a searing hot ray.

She flopped down on to the path and tingled all over. She felt herself growing and growing until she was four times bigger. The pelican was delighted. Being big would mean being even more fearsome. She spread her wings and hissed at her prey.

The rat cried out and ran, but the giant pelican gave chase around the mountainside. The boy followed, but she was too powerful. The rat turned and dived into a slit in the side of the mountain. The pelican tried to follow but she was now too big and became firmly wedged.

The rat stood in front of her, pointing, laughing, and sticking out his tongue. Maybe being big wasn't all that great after all.

Chapter Twenty-Five

The next morning, twenty-four hours before the start of the World Peace Summit, the newly ice-cream-loving Malevolo took the Dreadcraft out for a test flight. Dad, Danny, and Earl stood outside the lair and watched as it looped high into the air, soaring over the mountain tops and disappearing into the horizon in a matter of seconds.

Dad hopped around like a kangaroo on a sugar rush, while Danny watched carefully. There had to be something that made it zoom off like that. If he could figure out what it was, he might be able to disable it and stop them flying to the Summit. Plus, he could use it in his own craft to stop it from smashing into the mountain.

Afterwards, Danny and Earl pored over the blueprints of the ship, trying to find the secret ingredient. The blueprints were incredibly detailed and everything on them was labelled, with a breakdown of all of the components. Except one thing. Detail about the small green box with **CLASSIFIED** written on it.

'We have to investigate it and see if it is what we're

after,' said Danny. 'We need to get inside that ship.'

They sat and pondered their next move. Earl had noticed that Malevolo kept a set of keys in his jacket pocket all the time. If they could get close enough to borrow them, they would be able to get inside.

'Wait, I've had an idea,' said Danny. 'Earl, do you know where the boiler room is?'

'Are you kidding?' said Earl. 'My mum LIVES there!'

'Good, well maybe you can pay her a visit and help save the world at the same time,' said Danny.

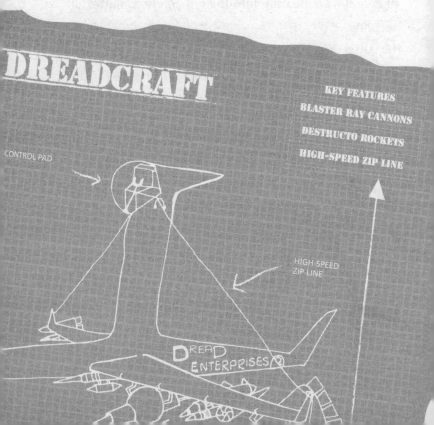

DREADCRAFT

CONTROL PAD

KEY FEATURES
BLASTER RAY CANNONS
DESTRUCTO ROCKETS
HIGH-SPEED ZIP LINE

HIGH-SPEED
ZIP LINE

DREAD
ENTERPRISES

Chapter Twenty-Six

'This is it,' said Dad, striding around the strategy room. 'The big moment. We must not allow anything to stop us achieving our ultimate goal.'

Danny and Malevolo sat at opposite sides of the table.

Dad flicked a switch and the screen came to life. It showed a diagram of the World Peace Summit building.

'This is where these so-called leaders will emerge for the, UGH, World Peace Summit tomorrow,' said Dad, using a laser pointer. 'We will hover over this exact spot in the Dreadcraft. Now, you're probably wondering how we will get down there and nab one, given how tight security will be. And you're right to wonder that, because, try as you might, you do not yet possess my vast intellect. But I'm going to tell you. We will capture a leader without our feet ever touching the ground.'

He switched to another slide.

'While Malevolo readies the ship for a quick getaway, I will attach myself to a line and be lowered down to the ground at a fantastic speed. I will only be within range of the snipers for one second. In that second, I will grab the first leader I can, and spirit him away

to the ship, like an Angel of the Apocalypse. He won't know what's hit him.'

He grinned at Danny, his fingertips pressed together. 'And this is where you come in, my boy.'

'Huh?'

'You will be in charge of the line—of lowering me down as quickly as possible, and reeling me back in with the dirty politician. My life—and the fate of our evil scheme—will lie in your hands.'

Danny gulped. He didn't know what to do. If he deliberately failed, his dad would be shot to pieces by the army. If he succeeded, they would kidnap a world leader and brainwash him, and the world would be plunged into despair and misery.

He had to get into the Dreadcraft without them noticing. Then he could try and disable that line and find out what that green box was. As Dad went through the finer points of the plan, he began to sweat. So did Malevolo.

'Are you warm, Malevolo?' said Dad.

Sweat poured down Malevolo's bald head like rain down a window. 'Um, yes, no . . . I am if you are, Masssster.'

Dad took his jacket off, so Malevolo did the same. Danny smiled to himself.

Little did Dad and Malevolo know, while all this was going on, Earl was in the boiler room, cranking up the heating. Then, once the needle was firmly in the red, he scurried to the lab and tripped the security alarm. It was so loud, it hurt all three of his ears.

Malevolo jumped to his feet and pulled out his blast ray gun. 'I will confront the intrrruder,' he barked.

Dad nodded and followed him. Once they were both out of the way, Danny reached into Malevolo's pocket and took the keys. He grinned. Everything was going according to plan.

For now.

FREE AS A BIRD

The newly expanded pelican was furious. She had to get her revenge on that rat.

She flew around the side of the lair and saw her opportunity—the hunchbacked man had opened a window to let out some smoke. She waited for him to move away before she squeezed through and into the lair.

She stalked down the corridor and poked her head into a small room. She saw the rat asleep on a bed, its strange human ear, surrounded by hair, poking out of the sheets. She had no idea it was going to be that easy.

She flew up on to the bed and readied herself for the taste explosion.

The pelican opened her bill and clamped it down hard on the ear.

'YOWWWWWWWWW!'

She didn't understand it—it wasn't the rat, it was a human! But the ear was exactly the same!

The human chased the pelican out into the corridor. She tried to waddle away but she wasn't as slim as she used to be, and soon the human with the tufts of hair and bright red ear had caught her, picked her up, and stuffed her into the rubbish chute.

As she lay in the bin, surrounded by bits of broken aircraft and ice-cream tubs, she made a vow to get that rat once and for all.

Chapter Twenty-Seven

Danny and Earl woke up at six a.m. Dad and Malevolo had been up late the night before preparing the line, so Danny knew they would still be in bed. He figured that he should have just enough time to board the ship, carry out his sabotage, and get out before they had to leave for the kidnapping mission.

Danny sent Earl on a recce to check that the coast was clear before they headed down to the launch area. They silently crept up the giant metal staircase into the Dreadcraft, using the pilfered keys to get in.

The ship looked just as impressive on the inside as it did on the outside. Danny couldn't believe Malevolo had built this in just a week.

The cockpit was spacious and luxurious, with super-comfy black and red leather seats and a mind-twisting array of buttons and controls.

'I know we OFFICIALLY don't like him, but Malevolo is, like, the best ship-designer guy—EVER!' said Earl.

'I know,' said Danny. 'I can't believe that weirdo would have such good taste.'

Danny followed the blueprints to where he thought

the secret box would be. It was somewhere on the dash of the cockpit. There must have been about five hundred different buttons, dials, and levers.

'Hey, what's this?' Earl was pointing at a small panel below the steering wheel with **EMERGENCY** written on it.

Danny took out the bunch of keys and inserted one of them into the slot. It worked. The hatch opened to reveal a large green button which said **CAUTION: NITROUS EXTERMICIDE. HIGHLY VOLATILE.** This must have been the mysterious box from the blueprints.

'Danny,' Earl whispered, his big ear twitching. 'Can you hear something?'

Danny crouched on his haunches and listened. Silence. Except for footsteps.

Getting closer.

Climbing the staircase.

Danny and Earl looked at each other open-mouthed. Danny slammed the hatch shut, then grabbed Earl and belted to the back of the ship. The door wouldn't open.

In a gut-twisting moment of desperation, Danny dived into the utility room and wedged himself and Earl in between two cabinets.

'Hmm, how curious—the door is unlocked,' said Malevolo, looking around suspiciously and patting down his pockets for the keys.

'Where could Danny be, Malevolo?' asked Dad.

'I don't know, Massssster. We checked every corner of the lair.'

'I can't do it without him,' said Dad. 'He's my boy!'

Danny almost shrieked. What were Dad and Malevolo doing on the ship this early? They weren't due to set off for another three hours. He hadn't even had a chance to sabotage the line. He was just going to have to hide and try to come up with another plan.

'I understand, Massssster, but time is of the essence—because of . . . developments, the journey to the Summit will take longer than planned. We must leave now or miss our chance forever!'

Dad sighed and plonked himself in the co-pilot's chair while Malevolo flipped a switch to start the engine.

Danny and Earl braced themselves—the launch was so fast, it made their cheeks pull back as if they were smiling.

Soon, the Dreadcraft was soaring high above the ocean, leaving the lair a dot in the background. Malevolo's leg twitched with annoyance. If he hadn't misplaced the key for the boost button, they would be travelling much quicker. He cursed himself for not making a spare.

Still, it didn't take long until they were hovering high above London, where the world leaders were beginning their journeys to the World Peace Summit.

Danny thought if he could inform the Lionhearts, they could evacuate the area. He felt in his pocket for the communicator. Empty. He'd left it in his bedroom. He screwed his eyes shut and hit his forehead with his palm.

'How will we do this without Danny?' Dad cried. 'He was supposed to be lowering me down!'

'I will do it, Massssster,' said Malevolo. 'I will always be here for you.'

Earl stuck his paw in his mouth and made a 'blargh' face.

Danny giggled despite himself.

'Wait, Massssster. I heard a noise back there.'

Danny held his breath. That weirdo really did have excellent hearing.

Malevolo's shuffling footsteps echoed down the corridor towards them. Danny carefully stood up, opened one of the cabinets, and climbed inside. Earl sat on his shoulder.

The door to the utility room opened. All Danny and Earl could hear in the darkness of the cabinet was Malevolo sniffing the air.

'I . . . can . . . smell . . . a . . .'

Light flooded into the cabinet.

'Rrrrrrrat!'

Chapter Twenty-Eight

'Danny!' Dad cried as Malevolo led him into the cockpit. 'You're here!'

'Yes he is, Massssster,' said Malevolo. 'The question is how?'

'You left the door open,' said Danny.

'IMPOSSIBLE!' Malevolo screeched.

Dad gave Malevolo a look.

'I mean . . . yes. That must have been what happened,' said Malevolo, his piggy eyes never leaving Danny's face. 'Silly me. However, it does not explain why I found him hiding in a cabinet.'

Dad raised an eyebrow at Danny.

'Um,' Danny scratched the back of his head. 'I was in there because I wanted to . . . surprise you. That's it. Surprise!'

Dad's frown broke into a smile. A mixture of guilt and relief swirled in Danny's gut.

'Anyway, come, my boy.' Dad hopped to the back of the room. 'You are just in time to help us make history!'

Dad let rip with his best maniacal laugh. Danny tried to force one, too, but his heart wasn't in it. Dad was too hyper to notice, though. He felt on top of the world, thanks in no small part to what he was wearing—the Dread Jacket.

Constructed from luxurious blood-red velvet, with lapels made from the fur of a long-since extinct rodent, and adorned by skull-and-crossbones buttons that glistened deathly black under the ship's lights, the Dread Jacket was a spine-chilling sight.

It had been handed down from generation to generation. Zoltar Dread wore it when he blew a hole in the side of that volcano. And it still had the scorch marks from when Peregrine Dread started the Great Fire of London.

The sight of this jacket had brought fear to millions over the centuries, and if Dad Dread had his way, it was about to do so all over again.

Danny's brain whirled while Dad put on his helmet and goggles and fitted himself with the line. At that moment, Danny felt like the most important person in the world. And it was not as good a feeling as you might think.

He examined the line controller. There were two screens: one which displayed a live feed from Dad Dread's helmet-cam and one which showed a radar. A blue dot signified where he was supposed to land. It was Danny's job to get him there.

'Are you ready, son?' Dad yelled.

'Yep!' said Danny, feeling anything but.

Malevolo opened the hatch, sending freezing air gushing in.

Dad lowered his goggles. 'Time to make history!'

Danny couldn't even look.

'WATCH OUT, WORLD!' Dad screamed. 'HERE COME THE DREEEAAAAAAAAAADDDDS!'

He launched himself out of the hatch and began plummeting to earth. On the first screen, Danny could see nothing but clouds. On the second, the red dot that represented Dad Dread moved steadily towards the blue dot. The reel at the hatch spun faster and faster as gravity made Dad its plaything.

Danny was in the grip of a hellish dilemma— deliberately mess the descent up and risk Dad being caught, or do as he was instructed and assist in the kidnap of a world leader.

But maybe there was a third way. Danny studied

the controls again. He figured that a small adjustment would send Dad slightly off course—into an alley, round the back of the Summit building, which would most likely be empty. Dad would be zoomed away so quickly, he wouldn't even notice. He would just think he missed the leaders.

Danny took a shaky breath and, making sure Malevolo wasn't watching, gently pulled down on the control.

On the first screen, skyscrapers came into view. Danny's heart raced. Here we go—the big moment.

He pulled down again, sending Dad coasting over the skyscraper and down the other side. The radar showed the red dot going off course. Danny punched the 'rapid descend' button and Dad plunged even faster. An orange light flashed on the panel:

APPROACHING GROUND.

Danny gulped and hit the 'stop descent' button. He left exactly one second before hitting 'return line'.

He braced himself for the fallout when Dad got back: the accusations, the shouting, the twenty-four hour sulk which followed every failed scheme. He could cope with that. The alternative was unthinkable.

Even through the howling wind, he could hear Dad screaming as he got closer to the ship. This wasn't going to be pretty. Danny thought he was fully prepared for what followed, but he wasn't.

Neither was the terrified man in Dad's arms.

Chapter Twenty-Nine

Danny tried to look happy but in his head, he was screaming. He thought he had adjusted the controls enough for Dad to come back empty-handed. Still, the man Dad had clutched to his chest didn't exactly look like a world leader. Danny couldn't quite put his finger on why.

It might have been the fact that he had a big white moustache.

It might have been the fact that he was wearing grubby overalls.

It might have been the fact that he was carrying a sweeping brush.

'HA HA! We've got you, you scoundrel!' Dad screeched.

Malevolo closed the hatch and accelerated the ship away at top speed.

'What's happening?' the man said. 'Am I dead?'

Dad cackled, laying on the super-villain routine really thick. 'No, but you'll soon wish you were! Of which country do you claim ultimate supremacy?'

'Wha—?'

'Hmm, must not be an English-speaking country,' said Dad. 'I'll have to try another way.'

Danny hid his face in his palm.

'WHICH. COUNTRY. DO. YOU. LEAD?' Dad yelled as if the man were deaf. 'I hope it's a big one like Germany. If you're from the Faroe Islands or something, this will be more difficult, but we can work with it.'

'What are you on about?' said the man, his eyes darting all over the ship. 'I'm from Lewisham.'

Dad stroked his chin. 'I'm afraid I'm unaware of that particular sovereignty. Is it in French Polynesia?'

'Dad,' Danny interrupted. He could take no more. 'I don't think that man is a world leader.'

'Quiet, Danny, grown-ups are talking,' said Dad. 'Now, come on, worm, spill it. What corner of this measly planet do you rule?'

'Hold on,' said the man. 'You think I'm like a prime minister or something?'

'Oh, ho ho! He tries to deny it! What a pathetic attempt at self-preservation.' Dad was by now hopping from foot to foot.

'Oh, for crying out loud, my name's Terry and I'm a cleaner,' said the man.

Dad stood there agape. 'Well, if you're not a world leader, then what were you doing at that building?'

Terry sighed and pointed at his brush.

'Ah,' said Dad. 'So you're the president of Brushia?'

Terry turned to Danny. 'Is this bloke thick in the head or what?'

Chapter Thirty

'Stop the ship!' Dad bawled.

Yes, the penny eventually dropped that Terry was, in fact, just a cleaner.

'Is everything OK, Massssster?' Malevolo appeared in the doorway.

'No, it is not!' Dad yelled. 'This man isn't even a politician. I have no idea how this happened.'

Malevolo narrowed his eyes at Danny. 'Oh, really?'

Dad stormed past him and barked orders for them to follow him to the ship's conference room. Terry went to follow.

'No, I, uh, think he wants you to stay here,' Danny said to him.

'Ah, right,' said Terry.

Dad snapped his laser pointer in half and paced around the control room.

'How did this happen, Danny?'

'I don't know,' said Danny. 'I dropped you down exactly like you said. Maybe Malevolo moved the ship.'

Malevolo shot up, knocking his chair over.

'I DID NO SUCH THING!'

'Sit down, Malevolo,' said Dad. 'I know you did your job correctly.'

Dad plonked himself down in his seat and swivelled away from them.

'Maybe it was me,' he said. 'I'm no evil genius. I'm a failure.'

Guilt twisted Danny's stomach.

'Come on, Dad,' said Danny. 'You're not a failure. It's just bad luck, that's all.'

'I don't know,' said Dad, sighing. 'But now we must decide what we are to do with this "Terry".'

Malevolo leaned forward, his teeth bared. 'He cannot be allowed to live.'

Danny gasped. 'What are you talking about? He's just a cleaner!'

'He has seen too much,' Malevolo growled. 'He may go and tell our secrets to our enemies.'

Dad sighed. 'You are right, Malevolo. He could blow our entire operation.'

Malevolo smiled at Danny triumphantly.

'I'll let you take care of it,' said Dad, still facing away. 'I would only mess it up.'

'Of course you would not, Masssster,' said Malevolo. 'But I have no complaints about carrying out the necessary duty.'

Danny ran after Malevolo. 'Look, just stop. We should keep him . . . for, you know, interrogation or something.'

Malevolo ignored him and carried on until they were back at the hatch. Terry was sweeping up and whistling.

'Come on, Malevolo,' said Danny. 'There has to be another way.'

'Your father has ordered it and I always obey my massssster,' he hissed. 'Unlike some people.'

'What's happening, lads?' said Terry.

Malevolo scuttled to the control panel.

'No!' Danny shouted, but it was too late. The hatch opened and the pressure sucked Terry straight out into the open air.

Danny dived at the hatch and grabbed the line. He was about to throw himself after Terry, but Dad ran behind him and grabbed his arm.

'Danny, what is the meaning of this?' he yelled over the roar of the wind.

A wave of nausea surged through Danny. He was about to scream at his dad for what he'd done to Terry, when suddenly, the lights dimmed and a klaxon blared.

WARNING! ELECTROMAGNETIC DISTURBANCES DETECTED.

Malevolo ran back to the cockpit as fast as his stubby

legs could carry him. Dad and Danny followed. When Danny saw the cause of the disturbance, he could barely keep his smile to himself.

'Lionhearts!' Malevolo shrieked. 'It's the wretched Lionhearts!'

All three of them hovered in front of the ship. Mr Lionheart held Terry in his arms.

Malevolo took over the controls and fired blast rays at them. Sure enough, they were stopped by Mrs Lionheart's electromagnetic disturbance powers.

Malevolo scrambled around the controls until he found the secondary rockets. They would surely blow the Lionhearts to smithereens. Danny held his breath. The rockets fired.

Quick as a flash, Mr Lionheart put up his force-field, which deflected the rockets straight back at the ship. Another klaxon sounded as smoke poured in through the ceiling.

WARNING! DAMAGE TO HULL. TAKE EVASIVE ACTION.

'Everybody sit down and strap in,' Malevolo yelled. 'Dreadcraft: activate cloaking shields!'

The Lionhearts watched as the Dreadcraft slowly disappeared before their eyes.

'That is incredible!' Dad yelled. 'How did you do that?'

Malevolo smirked as he steered the Dreadcraft in the opposite direction.

'That is not the only surprise I have for you, Massssster.'

Danny gulped. He was relieved they had escaped the Lionhearts, but didn't like the crazy look in Malevolo's eyes.

A couple of minutes later, the still invisible Dreadcraft touched down in a scrapyard five miles away, leaving the Lionhearts wondering where the Dreadcraft had got to.

Malevolo led Dad and Danny down to the bowels of the craft. What he showed them shocked them both.

'Masssster, I give to you our plan B: the Dread Digger.'

He swept his shrivelled hand across a massive metal monstrosity—like a tank crossed with a giant excavator. Each end had a wheel with four vast shovels attached, designed to burrow deep into the earth. Danny and Earl exchanged worried glances.

'With this, we will tunnel beneath the World Peace Summit and take a prisoner from below.'

'Brilliant, Malevolo,' Dad hooted. 'Sheer genius. Come on, Danny, let's go.'

'Actually, my liege . . .' Malevolo stopped him. 'The Dread Digger is a craft for only two people. Danny should wait here and keep a lookout.' He gave Danny a 'know your place' sneer.

Dad nodded. 'OK, but that is an important job,' he said. 'You are VERY important, Danny.'

Danny nodded and tried not to make it obvious that he knew Dad was trying too hard.

Dad and Malevolo climbed into the Dread Digger. The roar of the engine filled the ship and within seconds, a hatch opened beneath them and lowered them down into the scrapyard.

Danny rubbed his temples. How was he going to stop this one?

Chapter Thirty-One

'I can't believe we're finally DOING it, Malevolo,' Dad cackled. 'Soon, we will be burrowing our way into history!'

Malevolo chuckled, slowly steering the vehicle into position. Once they were there, he pressed the big orange **POSITION** button and the hydraulic pistons pumped the cab into the air and lowered it back down nose-first so the shovels touched the ground. He nodded at Dad Dread. 'It would be wonderful if you did the honours, Massssster.'

Dad grinned a diabolical grin and pressed the big red button that said **DIG**. The drill whirled and churned the earth away beneath them.

'We're getting out of here,' said Danny.

'Are we going to fight an ACTUAL CRIME?' said Earl.

'We're going to try,' said Danny. 'Come on.'

They ran up the stairs and out of the ship, the door clanging shut behind them. Danny had to figure out a way to save the day without his dad getting caught.

They were halfway down the exterior staircase when Earl said something: 'Um, Danny.'

Danny looked down and saw a man walking a dog. The man's mouth hung open and his eyes bulged. The ship was still invisible, so he was looking at a scruffy twelve-year-old boy floating in mid-air.

Danny giggled. 'Um, hello, sir!' he said. 'I'm, uh, one of those illusionist magician people . . . Ta-daaa!'

The man didn't move. The dog growled.

'I really am!' said Danny. 'I can prove it. Let's think of the most random thing in the world and I will make it appear. Hmmmmm. How about a rat with a human ear on its back?'

The man still gawped.

'Hocus pocus abracadabra!' Danny pulled Earl out of his coat pocket and held him above his head.

'Hi!' said Earl.

The man's reactions finally kicked in and he ran away screaming, nearly choking his dog in the process.

'Well, that's hurt my feelings,' said Earl.

The Dread Digger burrowed through the ground, churning up everything in its path—dirt, concrete, spooky ancient burial grounds, you name it.

'There is something soothing about destroying the earth from within,' said Dad. 'Maybe one day we can burrow down into the earth's core and cause havoc with some magma?'

'That would be excellent, Masssster,' said Malevolo. The Dread Digger's control panel beeped.

REACHING LOCATION IN TWO MINUTES.

'What are we going to do?' said Danny, eyeballing the giant crater. 'They've actually burrowed under the Summit!'

'That's no biggy,' said Earl. 'Us rats have been doing that for AGES. Talk to me when you can smell an overflowing bin within a three-mile radius.'

Danny didn't know what to do, so he panicked and did the thing that normal people do in an emergency. He whipped out his mobile and dialled 999.

'Hello, which emergency service do you require?'

'POLICE, FIRE, AMBULANCE, COASTGUARD . . . MOUNTAIN RESCUE—ALL OF THEM!' Danny yelled. 'You need to evacuate the World Peace Summit immediately. Something bad is going to happen.'

The operator tried to ask who it was, but Danny had already hung up. He hoped that they would get the world leaders out in time, and that Malevolo would get his dad back in one piece.

**LOCATION REACHED.
BEGIN UPWARDS
DIGGING
PROCEDURE.**

Malevolo stopped the Dread Digger and adjusted the angle of the front shovel wheel. He had calculated, to the millimetre, exactly where he had to begin digging for the craft to emerge in the Summit meeting room.

'Here we go, Malevolo,' Dad said, rubbing his hands together. 'Time to finally get this plan started.'

The skull-and-crossbones buttons on his famous jacket seemed to grin as the Dread Digger ploughed up through the ground, through the foundations, through water and gas pipes and, finally, through the floorboards.

Tiles, chairs, and tables splintered into tiny pieces from the impact of the Dread Digger blasting out of the floor. There was total silence when the great beast fully emerged. Dad threw open the hatch and leapt out, ray gun in hand.

'WHO WANTS TO PLAY?' he screamed.

'I do,' said Mr Lionheart.

'Oh.'

Chapter Thirty-Two

Danny and Earl ran back to the Dreadcraft. The cloaking device was beginning to lose its power and it had become translucent, like a mirage. Danny reached into his pocket for the key. Nothing.

'Oh, you have got to be joking,' he said. It must have fallen out of his pocket.

'You're going to have to break in,' he said to Earl. 'Climb in through the air duct on the roof and that should bring you out in the cockpit. You can let me in from there.'

'Aye aye, Captain!' said Earl.

Danny knew they had to get back into the ship. He couldn't have Dad suspecting him of alerting the authorities.

Danny watched as Earl scurried up the staircase and jumped on to a small ledge, and then on to the roof. He hoped he could get the door open before Dad and Malevolo made it back. IF they made it back.

Danny heard something behind him. It sounded soft, like a bird landing on a branch. He turned around.

'HAIII-YA!'

The boot smashing into his face did not feel soft like a bird landing on a branch.

'You lousy Lionhearts just don't know when to keep your stinking noses out of things, do ya?' Dad yelled. He fired his ray gun at Mr and Mrs Lionheart until he ran out of ammo, but Mr Lionheart put up his shields, sending rays ricocheting off every wall.

Dad dived back into the Dread Digger as several blasts rocked the vehicle and broke off the front shovel.

He re-emerged with Malevolo's fully loaded gun, but never got to fire it because Mrs Lionheart overloaded its circuits and made it about as much use as a broken colander.

Dad screamed in frustration and threw it at Mr Lionheart but missed and knocked over a vase instead.

'YES!' he screamed. 'TAKE THAT, YOU STUPID PLANT!'

He ducked back into the Dread Digger. 'Retreat, Malevolo. Back to the Dreadcraft!'

'I'm afraid it won't start, Masssster,' Malevolo whimpered, desperately jabbing the ignition. 'We have sustained too much damage.'

'That is NOT what I wanted to hear,' said Dad.

When Danny opened his eyes, the world looked different somehow. Much more upside down than usual. And definitely further away.

When he finally realized he was being held by his legs the wrong way up fifty feet off the ground, he screamed like a banshee on a rollercoaster.

'QUIET, MAGGOT!' Crystallina Lionheart shouted.

Danny tried to do as he was told, but it was impossible.

'Who do you work for?' she growled.

'Wha—? I'm not working for anyone,' Danny shrieked. 'Please let me go.'

'Fine.'

Crystallina released Danny's ankles, sending him plunging towards the earth. This was going to hurt much more than the kick to the face.

Danny screamed and put his hands out in front of him as if that would help, but before he walloped into the concrete, he stopped. Crystallina was standing on the ground below him, holding him up by his forehead. Then he lost his balance and crumpled to the floor in a heap.

Crystallina kneeled on Danny's chest and poked him in the ribs.

'What are you doing here?' she barked.

'N-nothing,' Danny wheezed. 'I'm innocent.'

Even though he was terrified and in agony, there was still a tiny bit of Danny that was totally starstruck. THE Crystallina Lionheart is crushing MY lungs. I'm so lucky!

'What kind of innocent civilian has their own airship?' she said.

The Dreadcraft was now completely visible. She's got me there.

'OK,' Danny wheezed. 'I'm Danny Dread.'

Crystallina sneered and dug her knees in harder. 'I know about you Dreads,' she said. 'It was one of your lot that tried to blow a hole in the moon and turn it into a giant Polo mint.'

'I know,' Danny croaked. 'But I'm different. I think you're g-g-g—'

'SPIT IT OUT, SCUMBAG!'

'Great,' he rasped.

Crystallina blew her fringe out of her eyes. 'You must think I'm stupid.'

'Honestly,' said Danny, hoping his windpipe wasn't about to collapse. 'I've been following you since you were five. Not literally; I mean in the news. I cut out every mention of you and stick it in my scrapbook.'

'ARE YOU MOCKING ME?' She twisted his earlobe.

'No!' Danny yelped. 'My favourite thing you ever did was the New York Zoo fire rescue last year. And when you foiled that plot to knock down the Hoover Dam. Oh, and stopping the Explosos stealing all that gold was pretty good, too.'

Crystallina stopped twisting Danny's ear and eased the pressure on his chest.

'Well, if you're such a big fan of mine then why are you carrying out evil schemes?'

'I'm not!' Danny cried. 'I'm trying to stop them!'

Crystallina got up. Danny did the same. He ached all over. To be safe, Crystallina lowered her cryogenic shades. If Danny tried anything clever, she'd freeze him like a crusty verruca.

Danny sighed. It was time to tell the truth.

'It's me,' he said. 'I'm Mynah Boy.'

'What can we do to get this pile of dung moving?' Dad roared.

Malevolo's hands danced across the controls. 'The engines are unresponsive, Massssster. The only hope we have is if we can roll down the decline, back into the tunnel—that might knock them back into operation.'

'And how will we do that?' said Dad.

Malevolo's huge forehead furrowed. 'Rock backwards and forwards?'

Dad huffed. 'I thought you were supposed to be a genius.'

Dad and Malevolo sat there swaying, smacking their backs against their chairs.

'When . . . we . . . get . . . back,' Dad panted between whacks, 'we . . . are . . . fixing . . . this . . . heap . . . of . . . junk.'

Mr Lionheart tried to prise the door open while this was happening. Luckily for Dad and Malevolo, this had the effect of giving them an extra shove and, inch by inch, they edged back down into the tunnel.

Malevolo hit the ignition. Nothing.

He hit it again. The engine struggled and agonizingly wheezed into life. The back shovel began to blast the excess earth out of the way as Malevolo engaged the **ROTATE CAB** command so they were facing the right way. He moved through the gears super-quickly, knowing the Lionhearts were on their tail.

'Oh, why won't they just leave me alone?' Dad groaned.

Crystallina's mouth dropped open. 'No way.'

Danny nodded. 'It was me who had the summit evacuated, too.'

She squinted at him. There was something familiar in his lanky limbs and awkward manner. 'Well, if you're Minor Boy, where is my communicator?'

Danny started to hyperventilate. 'I-I left it at home.'

''Course you did,' said Crystallina. 'Where's that talking rat of yours, then?'

Danny blinked hard. 'He was here a minute ago, I swear.'

Crystallina sneered as she twisted Danny's arm behind his back and shoved him up against the staircase.

'Spread 'em, punk!'

'EAAARRL!' Danny squealed. 'HEEEELP!'

A window opened above them and Earl poked his head out.

'What is it, Danny?' he said. 'Oh, hello, Crystallina! Are you arresting Danny? Oh man, this is going to make a GREAT news clipping for his scrapbook.'

Crystallina looked up at Earl then let Danny go. Danny thanked his lucky stars for Earl's extra ear.

She smiled and wagged her finger. 'I knew there was something off about you, Minor. I could tell you weren't a natural superhero.'

Danny wanted to argue but thought better of it. Crystallina studied Danny and rubbed her chin.

'So you're a super-villain, but you want to be a superhero?' she said.

Danny sighed and nodded.

She laughed. 'That is so weird—I'm like the opposite!'

'What do you mean?' Danny rubbed his arm where she'd twisted it.

'It is so DULL being a superhero,' she said. 'You never get to be bad. Ever.'

'You mean, saving the world is boring?' said Danny. His brain was spinning.

Crystallina scrunched up her nose. 'Not boring, exactly,' she said. 'But once you've done it a few times, the novelty kind of wears off.'

Danny was astounded by this. 'I would love to do it just once,' he said. 'But my dad . . .'

He gazed in the direction of the hole. If Dad saw him chatting to a superhero, there would be trouble.

'I feel your pain,' she said. 'What is it with dads and them wanting you to be just like them? It's like—hello, I am an actual person!'

Danny laughed. 'That's right!'

He couldn't believe it—he was standing there as himself, with no mask on, having a friendly chat with Crystallina. It was so nice that the sight of the Dread Digger skidding across the scrapyard felt extra annoying.

'Right, now you've done your good deed for the day, I'm doing a bad one,' said Crystallina. She scooped Danny up in her arms and flew him to the top of the ship's staircase, super-quickly.

'Th-thanks!' said Danny. 'But please, can you let my dad get away?'

Crystallina gave him an 'Are you serious?' look.

'I'm begging you,' said Danny. 'He's all I've got. As annoying as that is.'

Crystallina huffed. 'Fine.'

'Ah, thank you so much,' Danny babbled.

'Don't thank me yet,' she said, and whizzed back down to the ground.

Earl opened the Dreadcraft door from the inside and Danny was able to enter without being seen. The Dread Digger clattered closer, with smoke billowing out of the back.

Mr and Mrs Lionheart were following close behind.

'Freeze them!' Mr Lionheart yelled to his daughter. 'Now!'

Crystallina rolled her eyes and did as she was told. She had promised Danny she would let Dad Dread go, but she couldn't just do nothing in front of her father. The icy Dread Digger came to a complete stop.

Dad hammered the buttons wildly. The outside of the craft was totally frozen and the controls inoperable. 'What do we do now?' he yelled. 'We're trapped!'

Malevolo hit every button on the dash. Nothing worked. 'I'm afraid we are trapped, Masssster,' he said. 'But don't worry, I won't tell them a thing.'

Chapter Thirty-Three

Danny ran down to the bowels of the ship and examined the control panel next to the Dread Digger hatch. There had to be something on there that would get his dad and Malevolo safely back inside.

'Hey, what's this, Danny?' Earl pointed at a button with a picture of a magnet on it.

It was worth a go.

The Dread Digger began to move, slowly at first, its frigid tyres grinding across the tarmac. As it got closer to the ship, it picked up speed and Crystallina had to fly out of the way before she was crushed.

'You did it, Malevolo—you are a GENIUS!' Dad yelled.

'Actually, Massssster,' Malevolo went to correct him but stopped himself. 'I am, aren't I?'

The door to the Dread Digger bay opened and they were pulled inside. Mr Lionheart tried to cling on to the bottom of the vehicle but the door slammed shut and he was thrown to the ground.

Dad's door wouldn't open. It was still frozen.

'Now what?' he said.

They could hear what sounded like the police and the military arriving in the scrapyard.

'There is only one way out of this predicament, Massssster,' said Malevolo. 'And I'm afraid it will not be pleasant.'

Dad grumbled. 'What is it?'

Malevolo pointed at a large red button under a protective shield in the ceiling.

Danny sprinted up the stairs and took cover in the cockpit. Something about the way that alarm screamed

WARNING! SELF-DESTRUCT SEQUENCE INITIATED

made him think it was best to get out of the way.

After the explosion died down, he ran back down to the basement. Dad and Malevolo lay in the wreckage of the Dread Digger. They were dazed but not seriously hurt.

Danny helped his dad up and back into the cockpit. They had to get away quickly. He had heard about the prisons they sent super-villains to. Not even Professor Escapo could get out of them, and that was basically his whole schtick.

'This is the police.' A muffled voice came from outside. 'Come out with your hands up or we will open fire.'

Dad and Malevolo slumped into their seats. The Dread Jacket was in tatters and both of them looked thoroughly scorched.

The Dreadcraft lifted off the ground. Bullets bounced off it like spitballs. With a press of the throttle, they were away, leaving the Lionhearts, the police, and the army helicopters far behind.

Danny and Earl strapped themselves into the third seat behind the pilots.

'How did they know?' Dad howled. 'The place was empty. Someone must have tipped them off.'

'Yeeesss,' said Malevolo, sneaking a dagger glance at Danny. 'I am beginning to arrive at a similar conclusion, Masssster.'

Danny gulped.

The city zoomed away beneath them and soon they coasted over the sea. Dad was devastated.

'How can we have failed twice?' he screamed. 'It's not fair.'

He slumped down on the dashboard and punched it like a toddler having a tantrum.

Red lights flashed and a klaxon blasted.

WARNING! LEFT SIDE-ENGINE JETTISONED. RUNNING ON HALF POWER.

'Massssster, what did you just press?' Malevolo shrieked.

Dad didn't need to answer. Malevolo already knew. He'd thumped the button that dumped one of the engines into the sea.

The nose began to dip. Slowly at first, but then it got worse. The Dreadcraft was losing height rapidly.

'Malevolo!' Dad cried. 'Do something.'

Malevolo's breaths were short and raspy. 'I can't, Massssster. The only thing that would pull us out of this dive is a boost of nitrous extermicide, and I don't have the key!'

Danny and Earl eyeballed each other. There was no other choice. Danny unbuckled his seatbelt and ran to the utility room. It was the only place he thought the keys could have dropped out. He got down on his knees and scoured every inch of the floor. The Dreadcraft's descent was so intense that he kept sliding back against the wall.

Then he remembered: the cabinet. He threw the door open and sure enough, there they were, glinting under the strip lighting. He grabbed them and ran back into the cockpit. Malevolo bludgeoned the controls but it was doing nothing to help.

'I can't believe the only way of getting to a button that will save our lives is with a key that you've LOST,' Dad yelled.

'I'm sorry, Masssster, I'm sorry!' Malevolo whimpered.

Danny froze as if he'd been shot by Crystallina. He had the key. He couldn't decide what to do—die horrifically or admit he'd stolen from Malevolo. Horrible death or Malevolo?

The ship's descent increased Danny made his mind up. He slid along the floor of the cockpit until he smashed into the dash.

'Danny?' Dad cried. 'What are you doing?'

Malevolo's milky eyes bulged.

Danny didn't even look at them. He fumbled with the green key as the ship fell like a hailstone. He tried to fit it into the hole, but the violent shaking and the roar of the failing engine overwhelmed him. He took a deep breath and forced the key inside the lock and opened the hatch. The churning, black sea loomed closer and closer.

Danny smashed the green button, which boosted the ship's speed and sent it swooping back into the air.

Dad screamed and cackled. 'YES! I can't believe it! AHH HA HAAA! My boy saved our lives!'

'But Masssster,' Malevolo breathed. 'I think this explains why I could not locate the key for that component.'

Dad stopped screaming. 'You're right, Malevolo. He twisted around in his seat. 'Daniel Mephistopheles

Dread. When we get home, you have some serious explaining to do.'

Danny sat down in the third chair. Maybe the horrific death wouldn't have been so terrible.

'This is bad,' he murmured.

'Very bad,' said Earl. 'I mean, what kind of middle name is Mephistopheles?'

Chapter Thirty-Four

The Dreadcraft spluttered through the entrance to the lair and landed in the bay with an unhealthy crunch.

Dad stood up and stalked outside, the smell of burning following him almost as closely as Malevolo did. Danny reluctantly joined them.

Dad Dread felt his dreams of world domination slipping through his pudgy fingers. Rage grew inside his belly. And not the normal levels of rage you would expect to find in a man who dedicated his life to evil— this rage was much bigger than that. If his usual rage was a storm, this was a hurricane, and it was about to hit Danny.

'TEFFLEHGGGLEFFHERRRR!' he jabbered.

Dad was so angry, all the words he'd wanted to say got combined into one.

'May I, Masssster?' said Malevolo.

Dad nodded and slumped down in a chair.

'What were you doing in the ship, Danny?' said Malevolo. His eyes glinted dangerously, like one of the sharks that ate Kurrkus.

'I was just curious.' Danny stopped and swallowed

the bile in his throat. 'It is such an impressive ship that I couldn't wait to see inside. Then you got in earlier than I expected and I was stuck.'

Malevolo's nose twitched. 'How did you get my keys?'

Oh, crud!.

'Th-they were spares,' said Danny.

'THERE IS NO SPARE FOR THE NITROUS EXTERMICIDE BOX!' Malevolo screeched.

Gulp.

'You stole the keys from my pocket,' he said, 'in actions befitting a common thief—not a super-villain.'

Danny looked at the floor. He thought if he concentrated hard enough, he might be able to disappear into one of the cracks in the stone. 'I found them on the floor,' he said, never lifting his eyes.

'A likely story. But that is not the worst thing,' said Malevolo. 'You have been collaborating with the Lionhearts.'

'VAHHESSANAKKAWATTA!' Dad yelped with a spasm.

'No way!' said Danny. 'You're talking rubbish, Malevolo.'

'Then how did they know we were there?' said Malevolo.

'I don't know,' said Danny. 'Maybe they could smell you.'

'You are in league with our enemies!' Malevolo yelled.

Danny thought about the Lionheart Communicator and his Mynah Boy costume, and gulped. He stayed silent.

Malevolo reached into his pocket and pulled out a tiny data stick.

'I have micrrrrophones hidden on the deck of the Dreadcraft,' he said. 'I think if we listened to the playback from the time before we set off, we might learn something.'

Danny's scalp prickled. 'That's ridiculous. Why do you think that?'

Malevolo moved over to a control panel and inserted the stick. 'Let's just say I've got a hunch.'

'I think the technical term is "curvature of the spine",' Earl whispered.

Malevolo shot a look at Danny and smirked. He pressed play. There was nothing but a low humming noise. Then the voices started.

'*I know we OFFICIALLY don't like him, but Malevolo is, like, the best ship-designer guy EVER.*'

'*I know. I can't believe that weirdo would have such good taste.*'

Dad's mouth flapped like a fish that had flipped out of its bowl.

'Just as I suspected,' said Malevolo. 'The rrrrat can speak.'

Earl looked at Danny with fear in his eyes.

'N-no he can't,' said Danny.

'How can you deny it?' Malevolo waddled closer to them. 'We all heard him.'

Danny had an idea—what would Mynah Boy do?

'Malevolo is, like, the best ship-designer guy EVER,' he said, in a perfect impersonation of Earl.

Malevolo's face fell. 'So you were talking to yourself?'

'Yep,' said Danny. 'I just pretend the rat can talk. Makes things a bit more interesting.'

Malevolo's nostrils twitched. 'I don't believe you.' He turned to Dad. 'And besides, none of this explains why you tried to save that cleaner.'

Dad touched the tattered remains of the Dread Jacket and winced. Danny's mouth went dry.

Malevolo thought back to his own depraved childhood. Whenever he disobeyed his superiors, they would punish him severely—make him stroke fluffy kittens, eat candy floss, hug a teddy bear. He shuddered at the memories.

'While Danny is thinking about how he came across my keys and why he tried to save the cleaner, perhaps we should take in the rrrrat for observation, Masssster,' said Malevolo. 'To see if young Danny is telling the truth about that, at least.'

Danny and Earl exchanged a panicked glance.

'That is, unless Danny will admit to what he has done?' said Malevolo.

Danny looked up from the floor. He felt awful about letting his dad down and wasn't about to make it worse by telling him everything. 'Bum off, Malevolo'

Malevolo swallowed his anger and smiled that ugly smile. 'Very well,' he said. 'If you won't talk, let's see if the rrrrat will.'

He lunged forward, thrust his bony hand into Danny's pocket, and pulled out Earl.

'Hey, let go of him!' Danny made a grab, but Malevolo scuttled away. He reached into a cupboard, pulled out a cage and placed it on a workbench. Danny went for Earl again, but Malevolo dodged and flicked a switch on the side of the cage. Earl, sensing an opportunity, took a huge bite out of Malevolo's index finger. He retched. Malevolo tasted like farty cabbages.

Danny made a grab at the cage, but the switch had activated an electrical current, which threw him back against the wall. As he picked himself up, Malevolo dropped Earl into the cage, where his big ear sizzled against the bars.

'Why are you letting him do this?' Danny yelled at Dad.

Dad just stared at the ground and gripped the arms of his throne.

Malevolo put on a pair of protective gloves and picked up the cage. Danny ran at him but the twitchy little twerp held it in front of himself like a shield.

'What are you going to do to him?' said Danny.

'That is none of your concern, young Massssster,' he said.

Danny clenched his fists. 'Just let him go,' he said. 'Please. Earl is my only friend.'

Malevolo reacted to the word 'friend' like most people would to the word 'torture'.

'Frrriend?' he said. 'If you were truly one of us, you would know we don't have frrrrriends.'

Danny stepped forward and leaned into Malevolo's face. He wanted to tell him that he wasn't one of them and he never would be. But that's exactly what Malevolo wanted. Danny knew he had to keep Malevolo under control, so he could stop him without anyone finding out.

'Fine, take him,' he said, giving Earl a look which he hoped would convey that he didn't really mean it. 'See if I care.'

Chapter Thirty-Five

Danny didn't know what to do. How dare that shrivelled slug take Earl? He had to get him back, and soon. He shuddered to think what horrific experiments Malevolo had in mind for him.

He tried to calm himself down but the walls in his bedroom seemed to be closing in.

Getting to Earl was going to be tough. Malevolo always kept his room locked, and even if he did manage to get in, Earl was in that electrified cage. Danny realized that the only way to gain access would be with some kind of electronic disruptor, but he had no idea how to make one of those. He hadn't paid attention during any of those Weapons Manufacture lessons.

He was about to give up hope when something caught his eye. His school bag. Usually when it came to summer, he chucked it under a pile of clothes and didn't look at it again for six weeks, but this summer was different.

Danny dug all his textbooks out and lay them on the bed. The books were thick and heavy and covered in a grimy layer of dust, but their titles began to excite

Danny for the first time ever.

Danny allowed himself a little smile. He realized that maybe the Academy hadn't been such a waste of time.

To be able to defeat evil, he was going to have to think evil.

Chapter Thirty-Six

Earl hadn't eaten since he was captured. His dreams were filled with mountains of succulent rubbish. He would cavort among the rusty washing machines and lie on his back and make dirt angels while his taste buds zinged with the sweet tang of mouldy meatballs.

'WAKE UP, RRRRRRAT!'

Earl's eyes snapped open. Malevolo loomed over his cage, tapping his fingertips together.

'As I keep telling you, you disgusting vermin,' said Malevolo. 'If you speak, I will feed you whatever you want, but until then, you will go hungry.'

He stopped and stared into Earl's eyes. The rat gave nothing away. He was too loyal to Danny.

'Now will you speak?' said Malevolo.

Earl sat up on his haunches and washed behind his two rat ears. His tiny stomach grumbled. He opened his mouth.

Malevolo stood on his tiptoes. 'TALK, DAMN YOU!'

Earl opened his mouth wider.

'YES!'

And burped.

Malevolo cried out and punched the cage in frustration, sending a nasty electric shock buzzing through his body.

Earl yawned and lay back down. Malevolo flexed his sizzled hand and stormed towards the door.

'Poo-face,' Earl murmured.

Malevolo spun round.

'Did you just speak?'

Earl looked casual, leaning his head on his paw.

Malevolo grumbled under his breath and turned around again.

'Sewer-breath,' said Earl.

'Oh, I'll catch you,' said Malevolo.

Earl smacked his lips together and lay on his back. The human ear acted like a mattress.

Malevolo opened the door.

'Dung . . .'

He turned back around. Earl was still on his back. He sighed and slammed the door behind him.

'. . . beetle,' said Earl.

He gazed at the door. He knew Danny would be coming for him soon. It was just a matter of time. He smiled, turned over, and drifted away to the magical land of sleep where he chowed down on all the spoiled meat he could scavenge.

Chapter Thirty-Seven

Danny shut himself away in his lab studying the electro-disruptor book. His brain whizzed with currents, volts, and wavelengths.

He refused to speak to his dad because of how he had let Malevolo take Earl. Not that he'd noticed. Dad Dread was in the midst of an extended post-mission failure sulk and showed no signs of emerging. News of breakthroughs from the World Peace Summit only made him worse.

Danny vaguely remembered some of the electro-disruptor book, but this was the first time he had really tried to understand it. In the corner of the lab lay a growing pile of discarded attempts. He couldn't even get enough power to disrupt a light bulb. He was going to need a lot more oomph if he was going to break into Malevolo's room and unlock Earl's cage.

He searched the book for something that would help, but he was stuck. He felt like he'd read it four billion times. But then he noticed a section at the back.

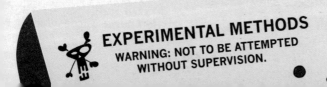

EXPERIMENTAL METHODS
WARNING: NOT TO BE ATTEMPTED
WITHOUT SUPERVISION.

There were dozens of paragraphs of different chemical combinations which would boost the disruption but with possible dangerous side-effects. Danny skimmed the pages, and odd words and phrases jumped out at him:

Electrocution.

Third-degree burns.

Explosions.

Nitrous extermicide.

That last one stood out to Danny. It was written on that secret green button on the Dreadcraft! Danny's eyes were glued to the text as he read on.

Nitrous extermicide is a new chemical compound, created by noted evil genius, Dr Gunter von Stassenbach from Hades Castle, near Stevenage.

It has hundreds of applications in evil and has been called 'the magic bullet' for all diabolical instruments.

It is as notorious for its volatility as for its versatility, though, and has been responsible for many deaths when combined with other chemicals in too large or small a quantity.

With blast ray guns: caused Dr von Stassenbach's lab assistant to explode in a big shower of goo.

With engine boosters: fired the aircraft of Dr von Stassenbach's next assistant into a volcano.

With electro-disruptor rods: created power surge which

made Dr von Stassenbach's next lab assistant burst into flames.

Further side effects are unknown because the lab assistant agency has stopped sending their staff to Dr von Stassenbach's lair.

Underneath, there was a table detailing the exact amounts of other chemicals to use with nitrous extermicide. Too much or too little and . . . *KABOOM!* Danny didn't care, though. If he didn't at least try to free Earl, he wouldn't be able to live with himself. He knew Malevolo must have had some nitrous extermicide because he'd used it on the Dreadcraft. He crept into the communications room. The TV was on but nobody was around. On the news channel, the prime minister said that the interruption of some amateurish super-villains would not disrupt the excellent progress they were making at the World Peace Summit, and that security would be stepped up as a result. Danny was glad his dad wasn't around. If he had heard the prime minister call him amateurish, he'd have flipped his wig.

Danny quietly entered the lab. There was a vast chemical storage unit taking up an entire wall, but it would take him weeks to search that.

He examined Malevolo's workbench for clues, rifling through drawers and cabinets, until he found a dusty red book with 'Chemical Storage Unit' written on the front.

Inside was a list of all the chemicals in the lab, in perfect alphabetical order. Sure enough, under N, was nitrous extermicide—location Z4.

The door for Z4 was about a metre high, with a big, stiff handle that screamed when turned. Inside, the chemicals glowed luminous green in their glass canisters.

Danny heard something behind him. Footsteps entering the lab. Without thinking, he hopped inside the cabinet with the chemicals and pulled the door until it was almost closed.

Dad Dread and Malevolo entered the lab. Dad was wearing his plain white coat again.

'No, he is not talking yet, Massssster,' said Malevolo. 'But it is only a matter of time. Once I apply some of my . . . methods to him, he'll become more cooperative.'

Danny peered through the crack in the door and saw Malevolo pick up a glowing red stick. A chill ran up his spine. *What was that?*

'Have you given any more thought to our next mission, Massssster?' said Malevolo. 'The Summit is still on for three more days, so there is a window of opportunity.'

'What's the point?' Dad grumbled. 'No matter what we do, the Lionhearts will be there to stop us.'

'I am working on it, Massssster,' said Malevolo.

Danny gulped. Dad's threats against the Lionhearts were always empty, but he knew Malevolo could have any kind of diabolical plan up his sleeve.

'It's no good, Malevolo,' said Dad. 'I'm simply too depressed to do any plotting. If you need me, I'll be in my quarters.' And with that, he flounced out like a diva.

Danny waited until Malevolo had scuttled out of the lab before he left the cabinet. He took a canister of nitrous extermicide off the shelf and hid it under his jacket. Knowing how volatile it was, he tiptoed back to his room with extreme care and gently placed it on his desk.

Time to rescue Earl.

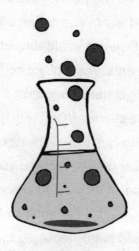

Chapter Thirty-Eight

Danny clutched his newly assembled electro-disruptor rod tightly as he left the lab. He had pieced it together using discarded parts left lying around. He thought he had added just the right amount of nitrous extermicide to the ammo cartridge, but couldn't be sure. He'd only know when he discharged it. If he had, it would open Malevolo's door and the door to Earl's cage. If he hadn't, he'd be too on fire to care.

He crept down the corridor, trying to keep the noise of his footsteps down. Being caught with a disruptor rod would be bad news. He couldn't leave it any longer, though. At any moment, Earl could break under pressure or else Malevolo would subject him to all kinds of nasty experiments. The thought of that glowing red stick made Danny's stomach churn.

He heard footsteps ahead. Oh, crud! He tried the doors either side of him but they were locked. He couldn't run—that would only arouse more suspicion. He spotted an air vent high up on the wall. As quick as he could, he jumped up and snatched the grille off, before throwing the rod in there and swiftly replacing the grille.

Dad Dread turned down the corridor.

'Son,' he mumbled as he walked past.

'Dad,' Danny mumbled back.

Dad stopped as if he wanted to say something, then carried on his way.

As soon as he was safely out of sight, Danny jumped up and got the rod back down. That was close. He took his Dreadphone out and dialled Malevolo's extension. This was going to be the biggest test of his voice talent yet.

'Malevolo?' he said in his best Dad voice.

There was a brief silence.

'Yes, Massssster?'

'Come down to the lab,' said Danny. 'I think I might have lost my contact lens in there somewhere, and I need you to help me find it.'

'Yes, Massssster, right away, Massssster.'

Danny laughed to himself after he had hung up. Genius? Give me a break.

He waited for a couple of seconds before carrying on to Malevolo's room. He listened to make sure the creepy assistant wasn't in there, then readied his disruptor rod.

He blew out a blast of air. The big moment. There was a small panel on the wall that controlled Malevolo's door. It could only be opened by the corresponding fob. Or a disruptor rod.

Danny aimed the rod at the panel.

'Here we go,' he said to himself.

He pushed the button.

WHERE PELICANS DARE

The pelican had been trying to escape from the bin for what felt like days. Every time she managed to squeeze her ample frame up the chute, another barrage of rubbish would knock her back down.

In the end, escape came in the form of a large, shiny thing, which picked the entire bin up and emptied the contents inside itself.

She tried to escape, but an enormous metal arm chomped down, crushing everything in its path. It was about to smash down on her. She panicked and thrashed about, and her beak hit a big red button on the wall which made it stop.

A human in a yellow hat appeared at the entrance. She heard the man speak: 'The things you find in the rubbish these days . . . this job never ceases to amaze me. Come on, big fella, over you go.'

He dragged her over the side

with a stick. She tried to flap her wings to keep herself from falling, but she was much heavier than she used to be and plopped straight into the sea.

The pelican resurfaced and bobbed on the calm waters. Being shut away in a bin had made her hungry for some fresh food and she was happy to find an abundance of fish flocking around her. It wasn't as tasty as the rat was sure to be, but her grumbling stomach meant she wasn't about to be choosy.

It was unusual to see so many fish in one area, though. Usually they only did that when they were fleeing from a predator. Something like a seal, or a dolphin, or a . . . SHARK!

The enormous beast clamped its jaws down on the pelican's tail feathers. The pelican cried out and started running across the surface of the water and flapping her wings. The shark followed, snapping at her feathers with its colossal layers of serrated teeth.

The pelican tried to take off but she was too big. She wished she had never been zapped by that stick. The shark got closer and closer, but she just about made it to dry land. The pelican turned around and gave the shark a mocking caw, before running straight into the cliff face.

She hated everything about this new home.

Chapter Thirty-Nine

'Danny!' Earl yelled. 'I KNEW you'd come!'

Danny laughed. 'Glad to see you're still in one piece.'

'Well, yeah,' he said. 'But I'm SO hungry. I'm going to be Rat Slimmer of the Year for sure now.'

Danny fired the disruptor rod at the electronic lock on the cage; it de-electrified the bars and allowed him to open the door.

'Don't worry,' said Danny. 'As soon as I get you out of here, we're getting rid of Malevolo.'

'Getting RID of him?' said Earl. 'How are we going to do that?'

'I don't know. Maybe I'll figure out how to trigger his ejector seat in the Dreadcraft or something like that,' said Danny. 'We can sort details later.'

Danny stopped and looked at his friend for a moment. He was so pleased to see him. Part of him thought he'd never see Earl again.

'What did that idiot do to you?' he said. 'Did he experiment on you?'

'He was threatening it,' said Earl. 'But I didn't say a word. I told you I'm the best at secrets.'

'Not any more,' said Malevolo.

He shuffled into the room with that infuriating smile on his face.

'You don't think much of me, do you, Danny?' he said.

'How did you guess?'

Malevolo laughed softly. 'As if I could be fooled by your poor impersonation. I know my Masssster's voice better than anybody.'

Danny rolled his eyes. He held Earl in his hand and eyed the door. He could easily outrun Malevolo.

'You have yet again proved yourself to be untrustworthy,' said Malevolo. 'And that simply won't do.'

Danny ran for the door, but he didn't make it. The last thing he remembered before he blacked out was a searing pain between his shoulder blades.

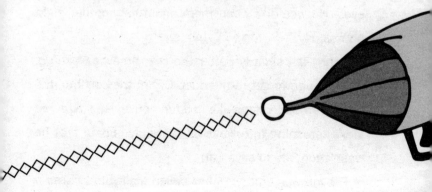

Chapter Forty

When Danny opened his eyes, he was back in his bedroom. He didn't know how he got there. For a few seconds, everything was fine—he was at home, in bed. Any minute now, Earl would probably stop by for a chat.

That was when it hit him. He couldn't. Malevolo must have zapped Danny with some kind of stun stick to stop him leaving with Earl.

Danny shot out of bed and had to sit back down. His head whizzed. It was like being seasick.

Danny kept trying to get up but his body wouldn't let him. He flopped back down on the bed and closed his eyes. He wouldn't open them again for another eight hours.

Danny felt slightly better the next time he woke up. Well enough to get to the door. Out in the corridor, the floor seemed to slope like in a fun house. He staggered along, crashing into walls as he went, hoping that he wasn't too late to save Earl.

The lab was empty. Danny called Malevolo's name— but he didn't answer. Danny limped over to Malevolo's workbench. There was something on there, covered by a sheet. It looked about the same size and shape as the cage Earl had been kept in. It smelled like Earl, too.

Danny gulped and steadied himself on the bench. What was underneath that cover might be unbearably disturbing. He grabbed the corner of the sheet and took a deep breath. With a quick flourish, he pulled it off and saw . . .

Nothing.

The cage was empty. Earl wasn't there.

Dad skipped into the lab. 'Oh, son, there you are!'

'Where's Earl?' said Danny.

Dad giggled and clapped his hands together. 'It is wonderful, my boy, truly miraculous. Let's put the debacle in the Dread Digger behind us. World domination is once again on the cards! Come with me and all will be revealed.'

Dad heartily sang evil songs as he led his boy down the stairs to the weapons-testing range. Danny didn't know what had cheered his dad up so much, but he didn't like it.

The weapons-testing range was a giant basement room cut deep into the mountain. It was round like a gladiator's ring, and separated from an observation room by two-metre-thick glass.

Malevolo was waiting for them in the observation

room. A red tide of fury gathered in Danny's skull and he thought about rushing at him, but Malevolo pointed at the stun stick poking out of his pocket and Danny shrank back. The memory of the shock made him wince.

'Why have you brought me down here?' said Danny. 'Where's Earl?'

Malevolo smiled, his green teeth glistening. 'Watch, young Masssster.'

He pressed a button on the control panel. Dad was almost bouncing off the walls with deranged joy.

A door opened at the back, flooding the range with smoke. The first thing Danny could make out was the creature's legs—long, thick, and cased in steel, like robotic tree trunks. The huge, hulking torso was similarly protected and the head was covered by a helmet which left only its face exposed.

It was a hairy face, with long whiskers and protruding teeth and—'WHAT HAVE YOU DONE TO EARL?'

'Calm down, young Masssster,' said Malevolo. 'We have simply taken the rrrrat and . . . improved him.'

'He was my best friend, you—'

Malevolo pointed at the stun stick again. 'You forget, we are evil. Friends are of no use to us. A nine-foot armour-plated rrrrat, on the other hand . . .'

'Change him back.' Danny pointed at Malevolo.

'Right now.'

'Impossible, I'm afraid.' Malevolo steepled his fingers. 'His genes have been irreversibly mutated.'

'Let me talk to him,' Danny said to Dad.

'I don't think that's a good idea, son,' said Dad. He gestured at the range, where Earl smashed a brick wall into smithereens with a single blow, then tore a crash-test dummy in half.

Malevolo pressed a button in the control panel and spoke into a microphone.

'Very good, rrrrat.'

Earl looked at the window. He gazed at Malevolo like a dog does his master. Danny wanted to cry.

'Now,' said Malevolo. 'Show us your special ability.'

Earl took a breath, then threw his head back and let out the most awful noise Danny had ever heard. Like a rasping scream, fingernails down a blackboard, and feedback from a speaker all rolled into one.

'What kind of a trick is that?' Danny shouted.

'Just wait,' said Dad. 'This is amazing.'

The other doors to the range opened and grey waves flowed in along the floor, quickly filling every available space. At first, Danny thought it was some kind of gas, but then he saw what it really was.

'Rrrrrrrats,' said Malevolo, his eyes filming over. 'We control all the rrrrats.'

Chapter Forty-One

Danny lay awake in bed, sick with worry. He'd made his excuses and left his dad and Malevolo cackling about their latest evil scheme. Night had fallen but Danny couldn't sleep.

Earl was being kept in a cell which could only be opened by a scan of Malevolo's palm and eyeballs. The disruptor rod would be useless. Not that Danny really wanted to be alone with the new Earl anyway.

He pushed tears off his cheeks with the heel of his hand in frustration. He HAD to do something.

Danny left his room and crept down to the cell. He thought he could try and talk to Earl through the glass and see if his old friend could remember him. Maybe remind him of all the good times they'd had. The only problem with that plan was that Earl wasn't there.

Danny sprinted up to the launch area to find the Dreadcraft had gone, too. How could that ridiculous Malevolo have created a mutant rat monster and fixed the ship in such a short time? He must never sleep.

Danny began to panic. With the ship and Earl gone, this could only mean bad news, and he wasn't around to stop it. He switched on the TV.

'And next, we'll be going to our roving reporter Liz Rafanelli, who is at the world's very first bouncy castle convention.'

Danny breathed a sigh of relief. Nothing bad could have been happening if that was the most important thing that was going on in the world.

'BUT FIRST, BREAKING NEWS!'

Danny nearly jumped out of his seat.

The screen showed London.

That's OK, a lot of things could be happening in London.

It showed the World Peace Summit building.

It's an important meeting. It's probably on because it finishes soon . . .

The Dreadcraft was parked outside.

Oh, crud! Cruddy cruddy crud crud!

'Shocking scenes at the World Peace Summit just now, as it appears some kind of giant rat has invaded the building.'

The camera cut to Earl, in full armour, smashing his way through a wall as police and army fired at him. The bullets pinged harmlessly off his body and didn't slow him down one bit. Soldiers charged him but he batted them away as if they were gnats.

He threw his head back and emitted that terrible roar. Within seconds, the entire area crawled with legions of rats. Grown men squealed like babies.

Earl disappeared into the building unopposed and emerged with someone draped over his shoulder. He bulldozed the crowds and re-entered the Dreadcraft, which then flew away.

'Bob, what's happening down there?' said the anchor.

'Well, Jed. . . Argh, there's a rat on my foot! Well, Jed, it appears that the giant rat has flown away with the prime minister of Japan, which is not a sentence I'd ever thought I'd say.'

'And where are the Lionhearts?' said Jed. 'Aren't they supposed to be protecting us?'

'Well, Jed. IT'S IN MY HAIR! IS IT IN MY HAIR? Well, Jed, they have arrived but it's too late.'

Danny turned the TV off. If he'd have known they were going, he could have called Crystallina on his communicator and maybe they could have stopped this happening.

He had to make up for it. He had to figure out a way out of this mess.

Chapter Forty-Two

'Who are you?' said the prime minister of Japan. 'What do you want?'

'I am the awesome master of the Dread dynasty!' Dad suddenly stopped and looked shifty. 'I mean, none of your business.'

Malevolo's plan had gone like a dream—leave early without alerting Danny, grab a politician, and back home in time for a lunch of delicious ice cream.

As soon as they landed in the bay, Earl had been instructed to drag the prime minister to his own cell. Dad Dread and Malevolo wanted to keep the prime minister locked up while they made the necessary adjustments to the brainwashing machine. Going from the London Ritz to a two-by-two-metre box with an angry mutant rat was a terrible downgrade for the prime minister.

Danny found Dad in the lab. 'What have you done?'

'Taken one step closer to fulfilling my, no, OUR destiny, my boy,' said Dad. 'World War Three will be in full swing by the end of the week. Isn't it wonderful?'

'Hmm, yeah.'

Dad sighed. 'I know you're annoyed about the rat, Danny, but look at what he has done! We have captured one of the world's most powerful men and we couldn't have done it without that rat!'

Danny forced a smile but inside he was shuddering. He knew his dad was right in a way, but he didn't want to be reminded of it.

Danny knew Dad and Malevolo were going to brainwash the prime minister soon. If he could somehow free Earl and change him back, perhaps they could both rescue the prime minister. But how?

Danny headed back to his lab and dug out his books. There was nothing in there about breaking through doors protected by fingerprint-and eyeball-scanners. He thought about physically dragging Malevolo down and using him to free the prime minister, but he was worried about that stun stick. Plus, Earl would probably tear Danny up like a snotty tissue, anyway.

Danny pored over the section in his book about nitrous extermicide again. Maybe he could use it somehow to reverse Earl's mutation.

Following the instructions, he combined a small amount of nitrous extermicide with some gene-mutating acids in a canister. It foamed and swirled. Could this be the key to changing Earl back? Danny sealed the container and ran down to the cell to see if he could somehow get that compound into Earl's system. But Earl wasn't there. Neither was the prime minister.

Danny gulped and ran up to Malevolo's lab. Too late. The prime minister was strapped into the brainwashing machine, smoke shooting out of the back like a geyser. He convulsed in the chair and groaned. Earl was standing watch.

'You're going to kill him!' Danny yelled, but no one could hear him over the whirring and zapping and Dad Dread's cackles of glee.

Danny hid his face in his hand—he was too late! Suddenly, the noise stopped. Malevolo scuttled from behind the control panel and unclasped the prime minister from the machine.

'Are you OK, Mr Prime Minister?' said Malevolo.

The prime minister slowly lifted his head from his chest. His hair stood on end.

'I exist only to serve the Dread dynasty,' he said. 'I will bring civilisation to its knees!'

Dad skipped around the room twice. 'And how will you do that, O faithful servant?'

'By firing all of Japan's weaponry at every major capital city in the world,' he said. 'And instigating World War Three.'

'What do you think, Danny?' said Dad. 'If this doesn't show the Explosos we mean business, nothing will!'

PELICAN GOES TO HELLICAN

You would think that nearly being eaten by a shark would have convinced the pelican that the rat wasn't worth the effort, but in fact, it just made her more determined to get him.

She waited until the boy came out alone, and then followed him back inside the lair through the open door. The boy seemed distracted and didn't notice her presence.

The pelican followed the rat's scent along the corridor and down into a large opening. The closer she got to this enormous metal thing, the stronger the scent became. In fact, the scent was much more powerful than it used to be.

The enormous metal thing moved and looked down at the pelican. She gulped. She thought getting bigger using that stick would make her scarier, but the rat looked like he'd been blasted about fifty times.

The rat sneered and picked the pelican up by the neck before throwing her out of the window like a javelin, straight into the side of a mountain.

Maybe it was time to find new prey after all.

Chapter Forty-Three

Dad Dread was more restless than usual. He was going to the annual League of Evil conference at Professor Destructo's lair in the Swiss Alps. He was leaving Malevolo with the responsibility of training the prime minister.

Dad had never piloted the Dreadcraft solo and was worried he'd write it off or park it on double yellow lines or something. Still, he wasn't going to miss out. This would be his only opportunity to gloat in front of all those big shots.

'Raise your hand if you've brainwashed a world leader,' he was planning on saying.

His would be the only hand in the air. And maybe that enormous pile of idiots would finally give him the respect he deserved.

Danny went down to the launch pad to wave Dad off.

'Remember, son,' he yelled. 'While I'm away, YOU'RE in charge!'

Danny smiled to himself with new resolve as he watched the Dreadcraft swerve clumsily out of the lair. For once, this was an order he was going to obey.

Chapter Forty-Four

Danny took a deep breath, counted to ten, and pushed himself through the doors to the lab. He had shut himself in his room for the past six hours, adapting a blast ray gun so it would fire his new mutation-reversal compound. He had to ensure that every trace of blast ray gas was gone. Even a minuscule amount would make Danny explode in a shower of goo. Still, Danny had figured that firing the compound at Earl was the best way to ensure success.

Danny slung the gun across his back and picked up a handy pole, which was lying on the floor nearby. Neutralize Earl. Save the prime minister. In that order.

Danny began smashing tubes and beakers, knocking over canisters and cracking screens. He didn't normally partake in this kind of vandalism, but it did have the desired effect.

WARNING! SECURITY BREACH IN LAB.

Malevolo scurried in from the cell, where he had been giving the prime minister a list of cities to bomb.

His face was twisted with rage.

'Stop that immediately, you vermin.'

Danny winked at him. 'You'll have to *make* me, Malevolo.'

Malevolo pressed a button on his lapel. 'Security to lab.'

The floor quaked with every footstep Earl took. Danny gulped and tried to ready himself, but really, nothing can ever prepare you to fight a nine-foot-tall rat in head-to-toe body armour.

When Danny saw Mega-Earl standing next to Malevolo, he wanted to run. But he couldn't. This was his only chance to put things right.

'Are you sure you want this to happen?' said Malevolo. 'If you stop, I will call off the rrrrat.'

Danny thought about it, then threw a glass beaker against the wall. 'That answer your question?'

Malevolo muttered something to Earl. Without hesitation, Earl hurtled towards Danny, sending benches and tables flying as if they were bits of lint.

Danny waited as long as possible before diving out of the way, sending Earl careering into a stack of barrels with a series of metallic clanks. While Earl picked himself up, Danny drew the genetic-mutation-reversal gun.

Malevolo scowled. He had no idea what Danny had been up to.

Earl ran at Danny again, but this time the boy stood his ground and got ready to fire. He aimed for the only patch of fur showing under all the armour—Earl's face.

Adrenaline surged through Danny's body. His legs shook. He aimed the gun.

Too late. Earl grabbed it with one of his enormous paws and bent the barrel, making it impossible to fire. With his other paw he struck Danny on the shoulder and knocked him into the pile of upended canisters.

Earl stomped over to Danny and grabbed him around the throat. Danny's vision blackened as the mutant rat lifted him high into the air.

Malevolo rubbed his calloused hands together. To see these two fighting each other, when they once had united against him, filled his shrivelled, blackened heart with joy.

Earl slammed Danny down on a bench and sat on top of him, pushing all the air out of his lungs. Danny tried to escape but Earl was too powerful. He snarled at his prey, his mouth dripping with anticipation, two sharp yellow teeth glinting.

'P-please, Earl,' Danny rasped. 'Don't hurt me. I'm your best friend, remember?'

A strange look entered Earl's eyes, as if a faint memory had drifted in from the back of his mind. He quickly shook his head, then dug in harder, roaring in Danny's face.

'Earl,' Danny yelled over the noise. 'We were going to leave, remember? We were going to Rat Heaven.'

The look came back.

He loosened his grip on Danny, but he was still stuck. A memory flashed into Danny's mind. Something Crystallina did to him that really hurt. He reached around Earl's back and twisted his giant human ear. Earl shrieked and sat up, pawing at his wound. Danny scrambled away. Malevolo was hopping mad.

'No, rrrrat! Do as I say and DESTROY THE BOY!'

Earl leapt from the bench and homed in on his victim. Any thoughts of Rat Heaven were gone from his mind. All he wanted to taste now was juicy human flesh.

He licked his lips and stomped his enormous feet. He let out another ear-exploding scream and charged at Danny.

Danny had barely any energy left. Another attack from Earl and he would be a goner. He looked down. The mutation-reversal gun lay at his feet, the barrel twisted. He knew he couldn't fire it, but that didn't mean the ammo was useless. It was worth a go.

He grabbed the gun and yanked out the mutation-reversal capsule.

Earl threw his arms out wide and roared. Danny gripped the capsule tight and threw it as hard as he could at the rat's open mouth. The glass smashed on Earl's teeth and the bright green chemicals inside whooshed down his throat. Earl didn't quite know what happened. One second he was charging at his prey, about to devour him; the next, this awful green goo was exploding in his mouth.

All over his body, he felt tingly. Just a little at first, but then it got stronger, like that kind of awful pins and needles he got when he'd been hanging over the side of the bin gorging himself on mouldy rubbish. It felt like his skin was getting tighter and his armour looser. It felt like . . .

'He's shrinking!' Malevolo screamed. 'What have you done to my creation?'

Danny shrieked with laughter. He couldn't believe it had worked. Right in front of his eyes, the hellish vision of doom that was rat-monster Earl was shrivelling back down to an ordinary rat. Well, kind of ordinary.

Danny dived into the enormous pile of armour and pulled Earl out.

'Are you all right, Earl?' he said.

Earl blinked a couple of times and smoothed down his whiskers. 'Is it me or did this room just get bigger?'

Malevolo stomped over with his stun stick in hand. 'Give me the rrrrat,' he barked. 'Now.'

Danny and Earl exchanged a quick glance. 'How about no?'

Malevolo growled. 'Because if you don't, I'll—'

'What is going on here?'

Dad Dread skipped around the corner. He had just landed the Dreadcraft safely and was feeling cocky. He only stayed at the conference long enough to have a massive gloat, before getting back to the lair and the important business of World War Three.

Malevolo hid the stick behind his back.

Dad surveyed the scene.

'What has happened?'

Malevolo pointed a trembling finger at Danny. 'This boy has undone all of my work!'

Dad saw Earl in Danny's hands. His eyes bulged.

'You did this yourself?' he said.

Danny nodded.

A smile broke out on Dad's face. 'Ingenuity and disobedience,' he said. 'You're my boy, all right!'

Danny blushed.

'But what about our rrrrat?' Malevolo whined.

'It doesn't matter.' Dad draped his arm around Malevolo's hunched shoulder.

Malevolo looked like his head was about to explode. 'But, why, Masssster?'

'The rat has served his purpose. We don't need him any more,' said Dad. 'Especially since we will soon have . . . the others.'

Malevolo sneered. 'Oh, yes. The others.'

Danny frowned. 'What are you talking about? Who are the others?'

'You'll find out soon enough, son,' said Dad. 'Now come on, let's get this place tidied up. As my grandfather used to say, "You can't do evil . . . in a . . . trashed . . . lab."'

Chapter Forty-Five

Danny and Earl headed back to their room after they'd finished cleaning. They still had the prime minister to save, but Danny was just so happy—he couldn't believe he had got his old friend back.

'I'm really glad you're OK, Earl,' he said. 'I don't know what I'd do without you.'

Earl grinned. 'I know what you want. You want a HUG.'

Danny scratched the back of his head. He didn't want to admit that that was exactly what he wanted. 'How about a manly handshake?'

'Done,' said Earl. He wrapped his paw around Danny's index finger and shook it.

Something bothered Danny, though. What did Dad mean when he talked about 'the others'? Were they planning to create more rat mutants? If they were, at least he knew how to create the compound that could stop them. But he couldn't help feeling that there was more to it.

'Did you hear them planning anything?' he asked Earl.

Earl shrugged. 'I can't really remember. The only thing I recall is being locked in a room with the prime minister of Japan and him finding me SUPER scary.'

'So you don't remember our fight?' said Danny.

'Me and you fight?' said Earl. 'Never.'

Danny winced and lifted up his shirt. Beginning on his chest, and spreading round to his back, was an enormous purple bruise.

Earl's mouth flopped open. 'I did that?'

Danny nodded.

'Oh, Danny.' His ears drooped. 'I'm so sorry. I don't know how . . . I can't . . .'

'It's OK, Earl,' said Danny. 'I twisted your ear, so let's call it even.'

Earl stomped his back foot. 'No, it's not OK,' he said. 'He had no right doing that to us. I'm going have my revenge on that weasel.'

'What, are you going to plop in his dinner?' said Danny.

'Don't you think I've already done that?' said Earl. 'I mean REAL revenge!'

'Well, we can start by freeing the prime minister,' said Danny.

He knew they were running out of time. Dad said the prime minister's training was almost complete.

Danny took his nitrous extermicide canister down

from the shelf, along with the acids he used for the mutation-reversal gun. According to his textbook, this same combination, with different quantities, could reverse brain programming, too.

The big difference was, it had to go straight into the bloodstream by way of a sharp dart. Luckily, Danny was able to use one of Dad's old ones that he had made years before to try and knock out an elephant. Needless to say, he had missed and the elephant had trampled Dad's old assistant, Sponph, until he was as flat as a pancake.

Danny and Earl headed down to the cell with their new dart gun. They peered through the tiny hatch in the cell door. The prime minister sat perfectly still, staring at the opposite wall. Without Malevolo's fingerprints and eyeballs, Danny couldn't open the door but Earl had noticed a small hole in the wall.

'Hey, Danny, maybe if I squeeze through there, I can bite through the cable that controls the door?'

'Worth a go,' said Danny.

There was one little problem. Earl's human ear. The hole was too small for him to squeeze through. They even tried coating his ear in grease but it was no good. There was no way of getting that door open.

Or was there?

Danny remembered a book on the shelf in his bedroom. It was thick and looked confusing, but he knew it might provide the solution to their problem.

ADVANCED COMPUTER HACKING

Chapter Forty-Six

Dad sat on the Dread Throne watching the news. His feet rested on the control panel and his big toe had worked its way through a hole in his stinky sock.

A satisfied grin stretched across his face. He was still buzzing after the League of Evil conference. They were BEGGING him for brainwashing tips but he had told them nothing. And to top it all off, he had finally humbled Mr Lionheart.

'To the people of London, I have this to say—I'm sorry.' Mr Lionheart now stood in front of the world's press looking less than his usual super self. Even his forelock drooped.

Dad cackled and wiggled his toes.

'We should have saved the prime minister of Japan, but we failed you, and even though we have now rid London of its plague of rats, nothing will make up for that fact.'

Dad laughed even harder.

'And things have just got even worse for the Lionhearts,' said the newsreader. 'While they were dealing with the rat crisis, famed evil family the Explosos broke out of prison and are said to be at large.'

Dad snorted. 'Typical Explosos, always trying to steal my thunder. And anyway, they shouldn't say "at large", they should say "at small". BA HA HA HAAAAA!'

Malevolo entered slowly. 'Massssster?'

'Malevolo!' said Dad, quickly swinging his legs off the control panel. 'I thought you were resting.'

Malevolo scuttled closer to Dad's chair. 'I cannot rest when there are forces at work that threaten to disrupt our entire operation.'

Dad didn't know what he was talking about but didn't want to seem thick. 'Ohhh, hmmm.'

'So it is my opinion that we should act first thing tomorrow morning.'

Dad shot up out of his chair. 'Tomorrow?' he said. 'But that's practically tomorrow! I haven't picked out an outfit, my hair is a mess!'

'It is the final day of the World Peace Summit, Massssster. Plus, the Lionhearts have been rattled,' said Malevolo. 'It will be the perfect opportunity to strrrike.'

Dad sat back down. 'You're right, Malevolo,' he said. 'Tomorrow.'

Chapter Forty-Seven

Danny woke with a start. He was having a dream that he was piloting his craft away from the lair. He could see the side of the mountain looming and he knew he had to press the nitrous extermicide button to get around it. He opened the panel and pressed it, but nothing happened. He opened his eyes just as the plane smashed into the rock.

'WHYAREYOUSCREAMINGWHYAREYOUSCREAMING?' Earl was violently jolted out of his own rubbish-based dreams by Danny's yelps.

Danny groaned and rubbed his eyes. He checked the time. Eight o'clock. He was sure he'd only closed his eyes for ten minutes.

'Oh, crud!' he said. 'That power nap lasted six hours!'

Earl shook his head to try and clear it. 'I don't feel much more powerful,' he said. 'And your face looks like Alphabetti Spaghetti.'

Danny checked his reflection. Sure enough, the keyboard had imprinted itself on to his cheek. He grumbled. Why was he wasting time having nightmares when he could have been dreaming up a solution?

The night before, they were sitting at Danny's computer in his lab, with the hacking textbook, trying to break into Malevolo's server in the hope that it would hold a code to override the sensors on the prime minister's cell door. It was hopeless. Malevolo had protected and encrypted everything three times over.

If Earl was still gigantic, he could probably have just smashed his way in there and got the prime minister out, but there was no way Danny was going to put him through that again. Even if he knew how to make mutant rats, he still wouldn't do it.

But being small isn't such a bad thing, Danny realized. In fact, in some ways, it's even better.

'Danny?' said Earl. 'You're staring at me. Do I have something in my teeth?'

'I've had an idea,' said Danny.

'HOORAY! Um, I think.'

Meanwhile, Malevolo scuttled about his room, preparing for his day of reckoning. A large titanium case lay open on his bed with two large guns inside. He knew he had to be extra careful with this Danny child. He'd had to deal with problems like him before, but none this persistent.

'OK,' said Danny, following the tiny print in *Advanced*

Computer Hacking with his index finger. 'You should see a green circuit board on your left.'

'They're ALL green circuit boards,' said Earl.

A few minutes earlier, Danny had opened a hatch in the side of the computer and Earl, after some persuasion, had crawled in. According to the book, it was possible to override certain security protocols by rewiring the circuits of the computer.

'This one should have zircon 8525 written on it,' said Danny.

Earl squinted at it. 'Yep.'

Danny grinned to himself. 'Right, now take the top wire out and plug it into the hole in the bottom.'

Earl carefully pulled the wire out and fed it into the appropriate slot. 'Done.'

'Now flip the switch from O to I.'

Earl did as he was told and received a sharp electric shock for his troubles.

'Did you KNOW it was going to do that?' said Earl.

'Kind of,' said Danny.

Earl made his way to the next circuit. He had to repeat the same process every time and even though he knew the shock was coming, it still surprised him.

'I hope this Japan man appreciates this,' said Earl. 'I mean it. I want the freedom of TOKYO when all this is done.'

Danny furrowed his brow and had another go at the encryption codes in the hacking textbook. This time, they worked. He punched the air.

'We're in!'

Malevolo shuffled down to the weapons-testing range for one last rehearsal. He took the special gun from the case. It was different from a normal blast ray gun. It was shaped like a cannon and attached to a small pack by a length of cable. The pack contained a highly volatile chemical. The same one that he had used for the emergency green button on the Dreadcraft: nitrous extermicide.

This version of the chemical was even more potent, though, distilled eight times to create the most deadly substance on the planet.

He pressed a button on his remote control and the doors to the range opened. A creature flew in. It was another giant rat, but it floated above the ground like a superhero. Malevolo turned his cannon to maximum power and fired. A green ray pulsed out and engulfed the giant rat. It squealed and twisted in mid-air. Within seconds, it was back to its normal size and standing to attention. Malevolo grinned. This superhero neutralizer really did work. The Lionhearts didn't stand a chance.

Earl emerged from the computer, his fur singed. Danny had finally managed to access Malevolo's computer system. Straight away, he started searching for clues as to how to open the prime minister's cell.

'Ooh, ooh.' Earl hopped on the spot. 'What's this?'

He bumped the screen with his nose. There was a file titled **NEW OBJECTIVE**.

'The door code might be in here,' said Earl. 'Plus, it might tell us what he's got planned.'

Danny nodded and clicked on it, expecting to see some kind of scheme involving a bomb or a destructor ray, but what he actually saw made his skin turn to ice. **ELIMINATE THE DREADS**.

Chapter Forty-Eight

'Looks like you're not paranoid,' said Earl. 'He really does hate you.'

The file was enormous. Danny felt sick as he trawled through it. As well as personal information on Dad Dread, it had everything about him, too—his school reports, his medical history, even a list of his fears. How did Malevolo get that?

'Why would he want to eliminate us? He loves my dad!'

They searched through Malevolo's system, scrolling through gigabyte after gigabyte of blueprints and ideas for schemes. Then they reached a folder called 'accomplishments'.

Inside were dozens of other files just like the one he had created for the Dreads. Each one was named after a different evil dynasty. And each of these dynasties had one thing in common.

'They've all disappeared,' said Danny.

The Destructors, the Cerberians, the Pillagers— every single one had gone missing in mysterious circumstances, and they had all taken on a new assistant who had helped them carry out a spectacular mission right before their disappearances.

Every case was the same—Malevolo eliminated the family, then took their best equipment. The rockets from the Dreadcraft came from the Cerberians and the cloaking device was from the Destructors.

'He's like some kind of parasite,' said Danny. 'He impresses them with his skills to gain their trust and then—BAM!—he gets rid of them.'

His stomach knotted like an old hanky. He had to warn Dad. Danny dashed for the door.

'Hey, Danny.' Earl called Danny back before he could leave. 'What's this?'

There was a file on the front page called 'Dread Objectives'. Danny clicked on it.

OBJECTIVE 1: Indoctrinate world leader using Dreads' brainwashing technology.
OBJECTIVE 2: Begin World War Three.
OBJECTIVE 3: Neutralize and brainwash the Lionhearts.
OBJECTIVE 4: Use brainwashed Lionhearts to speed up takeover of world.
OBJECTIVE 5: Eliminate Dreads.
OBJECTIVE 6: Buy ice cream.

Malevolo was going to brainwash the Lionhearts. A fire burned in Danny's stomach. He couldn't let that happen. Especially not to Crystallina.

Danny put Earl in his pocket and ran out of the lab towards his bedroom. He had to get the Lionheart Communicator and warn them. He hadn't used it already because he didn't want the Lionhearts knowing the location of the Dread lair. But this was an emergency.

Danny burst into his bedroom and found his secret box open on the bed. Panic stabbed his chest. The door slammed shut behind him and there stood Malevolo with the Lionheart Communicator in one hand and the Mynah Boy costume in the other.

'Looking for these?' he said.

Chapter Forty-Nine

'Give those back, Malevolo.'

'Explain to me exactly why I should,' said Malevolo.

'We know who you are,' said Danny. 'We know what you've done to other families and what you're planning to do to ours.'

Malevolo's smile evaporated. 'You know who I am?'

He dropped the communicator into his pocket and pulled out Danny's secret book.

'Not only are you a poor excuse for an evil genius, but you are also a TRAITOR.'

Danny's face burned. There was no getting out of this.

'Page after page of hero worship for this pathetic GIRL.' Malevolo tore through the book. 'And then this.' He jabbed a finger at a doodle of Mynah Boy, Earl, and Crystallina blasting a cartoon Malevolo with rockets. 'You have betrayed your family name again and again.'

'I'd rather be a traitor than a murderer,' Danny growled.

Malevolo stomped up closer to Danny. 'I will NOT be SLANDERED by a TRAITOR,' he said.

'Hey, come on Malevolo, don't be a JERK,' Earl yelled.

Malevolo's eyes homed in on Earl. 'And how could I forget the collaborator's trusty sidekick, the talking rrrrat?'

Danny decided to run. If he could reach Dad, he could tell him everything.

The blast ray ricocheted off the wall above Danny's head.

'That was a warning.' The gun smoked in Malevolo's hand. 'Next time, I will not miss.'

Malevolo led Danny and Earl downstairs to the cell, the barrel of the blaster never leaving Danny's back. 'Utter a single word and I will blast you to hell,' he hissed into his ear.

When they reached the cell, Malevolo let the prime minister out and forced Danny and Earl inside.

'Wait here until we have done our duty,' said Malevolo.

'You won't get away with this,' said Danny.

'Oh, I will,' Malevolo replied. 'Who is going to stop me?'

Danny stared at the floor. He didn't want to admit he was powerless. The prime minister gazed straight ahead, his face completely expressionless.

Malevolo sneered. 'But look on the bright side. At least you won't have to deal with your father's anger. Because he won't be coming back.'

'WHAT?'

'I was planning on keeping him around for longer. However, thanks to your actions, it would be better if I ended things today. But ressst assured, young massssster, Dread will die knowing what a disgrace his son is.'

Danny ran at Malevolo, but he found the cell door slammed in his face.

Danny threw himself at every surface, desperate to escape. It was hopeless. Malevolo was going to kill Dad, take out the Lionhearts, and destroy the world, and the only person who could do anything about it was trapped in a tiny cell.

Chapter Fifty

Danny paced from wall to wall—exactly two steps each way.

'Come on, Danny, slow down,' said Earl. 'You're making me seasick.'

Danny stopped and buried his face in his hands. 'This is awful.'

'Ah, things could be worse,' said Earl.

'How?' said Danny. 'How could things be worse? The world is about to descend into all-out war, the Lionhearts are going to become mindless evil drones, and my dad is about to be killed right after he finds out that I am a secret superhero, so please explain how this could possibly be worse.'

Earl shrugged. 'One of us could have farted.'

Danny sank down to the floor. He tried to force himself not to cry.

'Listen, Danny,' said Earl. 'There has to be a solution.'

Danny scanned the four solid steel walls. 'No, there isn't. Not this time.'

Earl scurried out of Danny's jacket pocket and jumped on to Danny's knees so that he was looking straight into his friend's eyes.

'When they turned me into a monster, it didn't look like there was going to be any way back from that, did it?'

'No, but . . .'

'But NOTHING,' said Earl. 'The point is, you did it. Look at me, I'm still here. Now come on, think. How are we going to get out of this?'

Danny rubbed his forehead. 'I'm too angry to think.'

Earl jumped off Danny's knees and danced around the cell on his back legs. 'Good, anger is good, let's work with that. SCREAM, that'll get it out.'

'Leave it out, Earl,' said Danny.

Earl carried on dancing. 'No way,' he said. 'Come on, I'll go first.' He cleared his throat, then threw his head back and let this weird noise out, kind of like the one he made when he was a super-mutant, but a hundred times quieter.

Danny screwed his eyes shut. The last thing he needed in such an enclosed space was that racket. It was too piercing to tune out. But he thought he heard another noise. It sounded like scratching.

'Earl,' he said. 'Shut up a minute.'

Earl stopped screaming. 'I feel better now,' he said. 'Well, my throat doesn't but—'

Danny shushed him and listened. There was that

scratching noise again. It sounded like it was coming from outside the cell. He stood up and peered out of the tiny window. Nothing there. Maybe he was hearing things. But then a grey flash on the floor caught his eye. A rat.

'Looks like one of your brothers is trying to get in,' said Danny.

Earl crawled up Danny's leg and balanced on his shoulder. 'I'll have you know that is not my brother,' he said. 'Nor is it a male . . . Hello, sweetheart.' He blew a kiss through the window.

A thought came to Danny. He remembered how mutant-hulk-Earl had attracted all those rats before. Maybe he still had that ability.

'As much as I'm going to regret asking this, can you do that scream again?' said Danny.

'All right, but I don't want to attract any dudes,' said Earl. 'Less competition.'

Danny shook his head. 'I reckon we could get them to crawl under the floorboards and bite through the cable that controls the door. I mean, they don't have ears on their backs so they should fit.'

Earl shimmied back down on to the floor. 'Sometimes your comments hurt my feelings.'

'Just hurry up,' said Danny. 'She looks like she's getting bored.'

Earl beat his chest with his fists and shook himself down like a boxer getting ready to fight. He took a deep breath and made the same noise again, putting a little more volume into it this time. Soon, two more rats appeared.

'I think it might be working,' said Danny. 'Keep going!'

Earl felt all his blood rushing to his head but carried on screaming. The first rat disappeared into a hole in the wall, quickly followed by the others. Little did Danny know, they were actually responding to an ancient rat language that went back millennia and is understood by rodents all over the world. If you ever see a rat in the street, it is not just squeaking, it is saying to its friends, 'Get over here, someone has dropped their chips,' or something like that.

What Earl was saying was much more profound, though:

'Rat brothers and rat sisters—I command you to join together and help a rodent in need. Burrow beneath the floor until you find a thick cable. Use your sharp, ratty teeth to gnaw through it until it has completely snapped. Then, when you have done that, go and do your toilet business on Malevolo's pillow!'

The door jerked slightly, then slid open an inch.

Danny sprang forward and grabbed the edge before it could close again. Earl urged his hordes to keep chewing.

The door edged open a little more. Danny pulled with all his strength as Earl's army chewed on the thick, tough cable below. Shaking with the effort, he prised the door open enough to squeeze through, then held it open for Earl. As soon as Earl shimmied through, he let go, and the door slammed back into place. Earl shouted a quick word of thanks to his comrades and they were away.

The TV had been left on in the lab. The news showed the prime minister of Japan arriving back at the World Peace Summit. Reporters followed him, asking how he had found his way back, but he brushed them off and marched straight into the building.

'We're too late,' said Danny.

'No, we're not,' said Earl. 'We have that plane, remember?'

'You mean the plane that crashed into the side of the mountain?' said Danny. 'No, thanks.'

'Well, what difference does it make?' said Earl. 'If Malevolo's plan works, you and me are goners anyway.'

'Good point,' said Danny. 'Let's go.'

'Wait.' Earl waved him back. 'We can't have you being seen by your dad, can we?'

Danny nodded. This wasn't a job for Danny Dread.

This was a job for Minor Boy, sorry, Mynah Boy.

Chapter Fifty-One

Danny and Earl stood outside their plane in the mini launch bay outside the lair. They had tried to bash some of the dents out, but it still looked about as flyable as a brick kite, even with the new nitrous extermicide boosters they had added.

Danny threw the brainwashing-reversal dart gun into the back of the plane and took a deep breath.

'Well . . . here we go,' said Earl.

Danny nodded and gulped.

'Whatever happens,' said Earl. 'I'm really glad we got the chance to be friends.'

Danny looked down at him and smiled. 'Me, too.' He crouched and held his hand out. Earl jumped into it and gave his thumb a high-five.

They climbed into the cockpit and strapped themselves in.

Danny started the engine and exhaled. The plane shook like a washing machine in an earthquake.

Earl and Danny gave each other a look. It was one thing launching one of these boosters from a safe distance, but to be inside the plane was another prospect entirely. How could the Lionhearts make the whole saving-the-world thing look so easy? It was terrifying.

'MYNAHCRAFT LAUNCH!' Earl yelled. 'LET'S DO IT!'

Danny pressed the take-off button and charged the boosters. The closest he had come to flying a real plane before then was in the simulators in Instruments of Death class. Which he had failed.

The engines growled. Danny and Earl gasped as the plane shot out of the launcher and into the open air. Danny hit the other booster and it surged forward, closer and closer to the side of the mountain.

He reached down and opened the panel. His fingers found the nitrous extermicide button. He couldn't press it too early or too late; like everything with that chemical, it had to be just right.

Danny's pulse thudded in his temples and down his neck. Earl crossed himself and said a prayer to ratty god.

The nose of the plane dipped slightly as the enormous mountain loomed larger and larger. Pressing the button in five . . . four . . . three . . . two . . .

The plane zoomed high into the air. All Danny could see was the clear blue sky. He had no idea how close the bottom of the plane was to the mountain.

A metallic roar shook the plane.

'Is it supposed to do that?' Earl yelled over the noise.

Danny hammered the booster again and the craft cleared the top of the mountain, a large chunk falling out of the undercarriage.

'WE DID IT!' Earl whooped as cold air whistled through the hole. 'YES! TAKE THAT, CRASH-TEST DUMMIES!'

Danny's laughter shook the tiny craft as it whooshed across the morning sky.

'What are we going to do, Earl?' he said.

'We're going to save the WORLD!'

Chapter Fifty-Two

Danny eased back on the throttle as they approached London. They descended below the clouds and a huge mass of people became visible. From Danny's viewpoint they looked like a swarm of ants at a picnic, but down there, a jolly time in the park was the furthest thing from the crowd's minds.

The prime minister of Japan had announced an emergency rally, where he was promising some world-changing news. Thousands of ordinary people, as well as the world's press, had gathered in Hyde Park to hear what he had to say. In his hand, the prime minister held a small console with a big red button on it. He had sent for it from his office. One push of that button would immediately fire all of Japan's weaponry at targets given to him by Malevolo.

Danny had to stop him before he could do it.

'I'm going to try and land on that roof,' he said, pointing at a tall building overlooking the park. 'I should be able to get a good shot at him from there.'

'Great idea,' said Earl. 'But I do have one question. Do you know how to land this thing?'

Danny grimaced. 'Not exactly. I never made it this far in the simulator without crashing.'

Earl nodded. 'Well, consider me REASSURED.'

Danny eased back further on the throttle and deployed the brake. He lined the plane up alongside the roof and pointed the nose downwards.

'Hey, it's OK,' said Earl. 'At least this will be EXCITING! Most of my kind go by chewing on poison.'

Danny slowed the plane down more. They were just feet away from the roof.

'Um, Danny . . . you have put the landing gear down, haven't you?'

Danny hammered the landing-gear button, but the wheels only partially emerged before the plane made impact, sending orange sparks flying past the window. Danny jabbed at the button again and the gear forced itself fully out. The tyres spun and the plane went into a skid.

'This is why rats don't flyyyyy!' Earl screamed.

The back of the plane careered towards the edge of the roof. It slammed into a gargoyle which plummeted one hundred stories and smashed into pieces right next to where Terry the cleaner was sweeping. The next day he handed in his notice and took early retirement. Luckily for Danny and Earl, though, it slowed the momentum of the plane and stopped it just millimetres short of the vertical drop.

Danny popped the cockpit open and jumped out. He pulled out the brainwashing-reversal dart gun and ran to the other side of the roof. He was just in time. All eyes were on the prime minister, taking to the podium.

'Ladies and gentlemen,' the prime minister began. 'Today is a day that will live in infamy forever more.'

Thousands of people watched in awed silence. 'During my time with the wonderful people who took me away from that so-called World Peace Summit,' continued the prime minister, 'I have realized that the way we live is wrong. We, as a species, have been foolish and misguided.'

Danny screwed his left eye shut and peered through the sight of the dart gun. It was so far away that a slight twitch or the tiniest gust of wind could knock the dart off course. He gripped the gun tight and focused in on the prime minister's bum. The gun shook in his hand as he touched the trigger. Mynah Boy hadn't had a successful crime-fighting career. It was time to prove himself as one of the big boys. He gulped and blinked hard. He couldn't afford to miss.

'This cannot go on,' the prime minister boomed into his microphone. 'We have to act to stop the world being irreparably damaged. So for that reason, the nation of Japan is declaring war—' He raised his hand above the bomb button.

Danny took a deep breath and pulled the trigger.

The prime minister jumped and squirmed. The crowd gasped as his eyes screwed shut and he clutched at his bum with both hands. Then the prime minister was still and a blank look fell over his face. He swallowed hard and cleared his throat.

'As I was saying—Japan is declaring war . . . on poverty, famine, and disease!'

'Did you get him?' said Earl.

'I think so,' said Danny.

The crowd roared. Strangers hugged. Even members of the press got a little emotional. Someone who wasn't as pleased was Malevolo, watching the rally on a hand-held tablet.

'DAMN!' He stamped his feet. 'How could this have gone wrong? I took care of every eventuality!'

Malevolo was a mile away, waiting on the roof of a skyscraper near to the Summit building. He had his superhero-neutralizer cannon ready to go and a blast ray gun strapped to his back just in case. Dad Dread was waiting on the Summit building roof with the same equipment. Malevolo was keeping him around while he was still useful. It might take two of them to deal with the Lionhearts. Once that was done, Dread could be dispensed with.

'Masssster,' Malevolo said into his communicator. 'I'm afraid the war declaration has not gone according to plan.'

'WHAT?' Dad Dread shrieked.

'We can still take the Summit by force,' said Malevolo. 'As soon as we have the Lionhearts on our side.'

Danny's shot had alerted the attention of snipers on surrounding buildings, and they all trained their guns on the roof. Danny and Earl hid behind an air vent. Danny folded his balaclava feathers down to avoid giving their position away.

'What are all these red dots?' said Earl. 'Oh, gosh— are they throwing a world peace DISCO?'

Danny's heartbeat kicked up a gear. 'I don't think so, Earl. I think some snipers think we wanted to shoot the prime minister. They are guns.'

Danny glanced at the plane. If they crouched and ran, they could make it. Maybe.

Danny picked up Earl and nestled him in his pocket. He counted backwards from ten, then sprang out of his hiding place. The red dots scrambled and followed him but he dived into the plane before they could open fire.

'Can this thing withstand bullets?' said Earl.

''Course it can,' said Danny.

As soon as he'd said it, a sniper blew a hole out of the back.

'Just not that many.'

He pumped the ignition and the engine roared into life. He waited for the thrusters to warm up, but then a bullet cracked the windscreen and he realized that perhaps they needed to make a move.

Danny edged the plane forward off the edge of the roof. It began to fall, less like a plane and more like a ball of spit. He jabbed at the booster button but it still wasn't ready.

'THE GREEN BUTTON! THE GREEN BUTTON!' Earl shrieked.

Danny did as he was told, and the last of the nitrous extermicide coursed through the engine and pushed them high into the air, away from the sights of the snipers.

Danny laughed hysterically as he steered the craft around buildings. 'Where would I be without you, Earl?'

'Squished on the pavement, probably!'

Danny levelled the plane off and engaged the throttle. He knew where to go next.

Malevolo watched the skies with a grim smile. He pulled the disgusting boy's L-shaped communication device out of his pocket and pressed the button. The intercom crackled into life.

'Crystallina Lionheart.'

'Aww, help me!' Malevolo squealed. 'Those awful evil geniuses are about to do something terrible on the roof of the World Peace Summit building. Come quick!'

'Who is this?' asked Crystallina.

Malevolo growled. 'Never mind that, just get here before it's too late!'

'Fine. We'll be right there.'

The communicator cut out. Malevolo chuckled to himself and pressed the button on his own communicator.

'Massssster,' he purred. 'The others will be here imminently.'

Dad Dread cackled. He wasn't going to allow a little hiccup like the brainwashing not working spoil his day. There was still the chance to get the Lionhearts. They would take the rest of the summit by force if they had to! Soon, the entire world would bow to the name of Dread.

Earl spotted the little round dot on the roof first.

'There he is,' he said, pointing at Malevolo.

Danny nodded and started to bring the plane down. 'I won't forget the landing gear this time.'

He pressed the button. There was a dry scraping sound but nothing happened. His mouth fell open.

'Even though you're wearing a balaclava, there's something about your expression that is slightly worrying,' said Earl.

'It's OK,' Danny lied. 'Everything is going to be fine. You just might want to brace yourself, that's all.'

He slowed the plane down and lined it up with the roof. He could see Malevolo watching them.

Danny dipped the nose and headed in to land. His heart thudded. Any landing without landing gear was going to be a problem.

The belly of the plane scraped against the roof with an ear-shattering shriek. It skidded this way and that as Danny tried to keep it going in a straight line. The good news was, he managed it. The bad news was . . .

'Oh, cruuuuddd!'

BANG!

. . . the straight line ended with a brick wall.

Danny and Earl were thrown forward in their seats. The undercarriage, nose, and tail of the plane were completely destroyed, and foul-smelling smoke spewed out of the engines.

'Yet another AWESOME landing, Captain Dread,' said Earl.

While Malevolo watched the Mynahcraft crashlanding on the roof, his mind raced. Could DANNY be behind the prime minister's change of heart?

Mynah Boy jumped out of the cockpit and assumed a kung-fu stance.

'Is that you under the ridiculous balaclava, Danny?! B-but I locked you up!' Malevolo cried.

'Shut up, Malevolo' said Mynah Boy. 'Your little scheme is over.'

Malevolo put down his superhero-neutralizer cannon and got out his blast ray gun. He knew the blast rays would be useless against the Lionhearts' shields, but a puny child in a jumper would be an easy target.

'I was right,' said Malevolo. 'You are a traitor.'

'Maybe I am,' said Danny. 'But I'd rather be a traitor than what you are—a parasite and a killer.'

Malevolo pointed his gun at Danny's chest. 'If you were an evil genius, you would understand,' he said. 'You would know why I lust for power. You would know why it is not enough for me to be a lowly assistant.'

He stepped closer to Danny, his finger twitching on the trigger. 'The Cerberians were no match for me. Neither were the Destructors. And the Pillagers? The boy had suspicions like you. But I . . . dealt with him.'

An arctic chill ran up Danny's spine. He remembered how Billy Pillager hadn't returned to the Academy after last summer.

'Your idiotic father is on the roof of the Summit building,' said Malevolo. 'He is going to neutralize the Lionhearts and brainwash them into doing our bidding. And there is nothing you can do.'

While all this was going on, Earl saw his opportunity. He clambered out of the crumpled wreckage of the plane and scurried around the back. The line between Malevolo's superhero-neutralizer cannon and the ammo pack was thick, but nothing his teeth couldn't handle. He'd just pretend that it was chicken. Tough chicken, but chicken nonetheless.

'Yes, boy,' said Malevolo. 'If you were truly one of us, you would understand, and you certainly wouldn't fraternize with RRRRRRATS!'

He spun round and caught Earl with a mouthful of wire.

Danny's heart jumped. 'Earl, run!'

He tried, but Malevolo was on him and snapped his wiry hands around Earl's body. Danny lunged forward but it was too late. Malevolo had launched Earl off the roof, his tiny body spinning towards the hard ground three hundred stories below.

As he fell, he shouted, 'TRUST IN YOUR POWERS, MYNAH BOOOOOOOOOOOOY!'

'EARL!' Danny screeched, but Malevolo fixed his blast ray on him.

'Now what will you do with no rrrrat?'

Danny growled and ran full pelt at Malevolo. He didn't care about the gun. Malevolo had just taken away the only good thing in his life. Malevolo scuttled backwards and fired, but Danny dodged the blast, constantly surging forward.

Mynah Boy was becoming Mynah Man.

Malevolo missed again, but the ray ricocheted off an air vent and glanced off Danny's shoulder. He stumbled backwards, the force of the ray knocking him off balance. Danny stumbled over the edge of the building and instinctively grabbed on to the gutter.

Without wanting to, Danny glanced down at the pavement below. His stomach lurched and his long legs flailed in the wind. People going about their daily business looked like bugs.

He looked up and framed against the brilliant blue sky was Malevolo, his gun trained on Danny's head.

'Time to say goodbye, young Massssster.'

Danny's breathed short and fast. 'How can you live with yourself?'

Malevolo growled. 'Stop trying to stall me, boy.'

Danny's fingers began to go numb.

Malevolo pulled the trigger.

CLICK.

'What's the matter, Malevolo?' said Danny. 'Run out of ammo?'

Malevolo grinned and pulled a single luminous green cartridge out of his holster.

'Nitrous extermicide,' he said as he loaded it into the barrel. 'One shot of this will blast you to Kingdom Come.'

Danny's mind raced. He'd read something about this when he was researching. His grip on the gutter began to loosen.

'I know what that is,' said Danny. 'And if you fire it through that weapon, you'll be sorry.'

Malevolo sneered. 'What are you talking about?'

'I have read up on all of Dr Gunter von Stassenbach's experiments with nitrous extermicide and I know how it reacts with certain elements.'

'Silence!' Malevolo screamed. 'How dare you, a pathetic worm who can't even pass his classes at the Academy, try to teach me, the finest evil mind on this measly planet, anything about diabolical science?'

'I'm not trying to teach you anything,' Danny panted. 'I just know that as soon as you pull that trigger, the blast ray gases will combine with the nitrous extermicide, and it will make you . . .'

Malevolo roared and pulled the trigger. Within a millisecond, the elements reacted just as Danny said they would, and Malevolo erupted in a colossal shower of disgusting green goo.

'. . . explode,' said Danny.

Chapter Fifty-Three

Danny took a deep breath and used the rest of his energy to drag himself back up on to the roof. He dangled his legs over the side. Malevolo was gone, but that didn't matter. Because so was Earl. The one person, well, not a person exactly, but the one THING that his made life worth living. It was Earl who made him believe in himself enough to finally become Mynah Boy. Now what was he going to do?

His plane was destroyed so he couldn't stop Dad, and soon, the Lionhearts would be gone, too. Replaced with mindless evil drones designed to do Dad's bidding. Anyway, he wouldn't be able to do anything without Earl. Whenever he was ready to give up, Earl was the one who would pick him up and make him realize he could do it. Without him, he was useless.

Danny hoped that, somehow, Earl was in a better place. He deserved that.

A single tear rolled down Danny's cheek and fell all the way down to the street below, where it splashed into the gutter like a raindrop.

PELICAN'S BiG ADVENTURE

The pelican sat on her perch and nursed her bruises. She had finally given up. There was no way she had any chance of taking on that enormous rat. She thought about going over to the Isle of Sheep—she was so big now that she could probably pick one up.

She was warming up for the journey when she noticed something by the entrance to the lair. No, it couldn't be. It was. It was the rat! And back to his normal, edible size.

He got into that shiny ship with the boy. She had seen how fast it was. There was no chance she'd be able to keep up.

When she saw it struggling to get over the top of the mountain, she flew up and grabbed on to the top of it, using her beak to lock herself into position. She beat her wings hard and helped it over the peak of the mountain. She wanted to take her prey alive.

Where the rat was going was like nowhere the pelican had ever seen before. The mountains were tall and square and had glimmering surfaces in them that reflected the sunlight and burned her eyes.

When the shiny thing started to come down, it shook the pelican off and she waited on a ledge . . .

She never took her eyes off the rat, but he was always too close to the boy for her to make her move. Then, when they went back to the shiny thing, something nearly blew her tail feathers off, and she had to dive to get away.

She flew full pelt to follow the fast thing, but she saw the little hunched man and hid on a sill underneath. She knew he was bad news.

Just as the pelican was starting to get comfortable, she saw something whizz past her. At first, she thought it was one of those pigeons, but the way it fell didn't seem right. It was her rat!

She dive-bombed off the ledge, tucking her wings behind as her long beak cut through the wind. The rat twisted as it fell. Seeing her opportunity, the pelican opened her beak and snapped it shut on the rat's tail. She unfolded her wings and swooped back into the air with the rat dangling.

Success! At long last, after weeks of trying, she had her rat. All the pain and suffering had finally paid off.

She flipped the rat on to her beak and looked into his eyes. She imagined how juicy he would taste. How succulent that ear would be. But then she thought about all the adventures they had had together. The thrill she felt when she swooped at him. The way her heart would jump when she saw his tiny face.

Maybe what was fun was the chase, not the kill. Maybe she just enjoyed playing with him. Maybe they were supposed to be friends.

The rat made a noise and pointed upwards. He wanted to go back where he came from.

When the pelican flew back on to the roof with the rat in her beak, the boy looked so happy. It reminded the pelican of something—a feeling from her old life.

The rat hopped up on to the pelican's back and held his front legs around her neck. Then he scurried up to her face and pressed his mouth against her beak.

The pelican didn't really understand what this meant, but she knew she enjoyed it.

Chapter Fifty-Four

Danny thought he'd gone mad. There, floating in front of his eyes was the friend he'd given up as dead, alive and well and riding a giant pelican.

'How the—' Danny stood up.

'No time to explain, Danny,' Earl yelled. 'HOP ON!'

Danny dragged his balaclava down, picked up Malevolo's neutralizer cannon, and jumped on to the pelican's back. She took off, much slower than she would normally, but still keeping a steady pace.

'Over there, girl.' Earl steered her towards the main World Peace Summit building. 'We don't have much time.'

The wind blew Danny's balaclava feathers. He had no idea who the giant pelican was or where it had come from but this was his last chance to save the Lionhearts.

In the high-rise office of Dr Susan Bergman, a small boy with psychopathic tendencies called Timmy was being shown inkblots and asked to tell the doctor what he could see.

'Devil,' he rhymed off listlessly. 'Demon . . . pickaxe.'

Then his eye was caught by something going past the large window behind the doctor.

'A boy and a rat riding a massive pelican!'

Dr Bergman glanced at the inkblot and shrugged. That was a new one.

A helicopter with mounted cameras hovered above Danny and his animal accomplices.

'Quick,' Danny yelled to Earl over the roar of the blades. 'Hide in my pocket. If Dad sees you, he'll know it's me!'

Earl saluted and ran along the length of the pelican's back into Danny's pocket.

'COME ON, MYNAH BOY—IT'S TIME TO SAVE THE WORLD!' he whooped.

Danny spotted the meatball-like figure of Dad Dread standing on the rooftop, wielding his superhero-neutralizer cannon. Even from that distance, he could hear him cackling.

Three dots appeared on the horizon. Danny knew who they were.

'Quick, pelican!' he cried. 'We're not going to make it!'

The poor bird flapped her wings as hard as she could, but they weren't going to land on the roof before the Lionhearts got there.

'Yes!' Dad screamed as the heroes hovered above him. 'Feel the power of the Dread dynasty!'

He fired his superhero-neutralizer cannon at the Lionhearts. A green fog engulfed them. They went limp like ragdolls as they entered a state of suspended animation.

People in the streets below looked up in horror. Their heroes—the only thing keeping the world from destruction—were about to be taken out for good.

'Here we go,' said Danny. He fired Malevolo's neutralizer cannon at the fog. He knew it was designed to suspend the Lionhearts' powers and, for all he knew, it might have just speeded things up. He just had to hope that it would cancel the other one out.

All over the world, people stopped to watch the horror unfold on live TV.

'It appears that a balaclava-wearing boy sitting on a bird has arrived on the scene,' said Jed Blatsky. 'We don't know who he is, but our sources suggest that he is crazy.'

The Mayhem twins stopped chasing the monster fly around their lair and gawped at the TV.

'It's Minor Boy!' said Matt.

'We've met a celebrity!' said Murray. 'Wait 'til Danny hears about this!'

The cannon vibrated in Danny's hands and his heart jackhammered. Toxic chemicals surged through a line that ran from the pack, which wobbled dangerously on the pelican's tail feathers.

The green haze that paralysed the helpless superheroes began to turn blue. Dad clocked the strange boy on a bird trying to undo his good work and cried out in frustration. He dialled up the power on his neutralizer which stopped the colour change. The disturbance dragged the Lionhearts around the fog, smashing them into each other.

Danny leaned backwards and cranked up the power on the pack as high as it would go, gripping the pelican between his thighs in a desperate attempt to stay on. The poor bird was exhausted but Earl willed her forwards, closer to the Lionhearts. The cannon beeped a WARNING. It was nearly empty. The pack shook so violently, it fell off the pelican and dangled by her feet. Still, the giant bird struggled closer. Danny could see Crystallina's face frozen in an expression of horror.

The fog became entirely blue, then got brighter and brighter. Danny's grip on the pelican became flimsier with every pulsation. Suddenly, the fog disappeared, replaced by a light that made everyone within a two-mile radius shield their eyes.

The pelican lost her bearings and tumbled, crashlanding on the roof and sending Danny and Earl skidding into Dad.

Dad threw his empty cannon down and looked at the crumpled superhero at his feet. 'Who the devil are you?'

Danny tried to crawl away but Dad wrenched him up by his collar. 'I ASKED YOU A QUESTION!'

His eyes flitted all over Danny. 'You look familiar.'

Danny's breath hitched in his throat. This could not be happening. His Dad could not know it was he who had wrecked his plan.

His eyes wide like plates, Dad grabbed the bottom of Mynah Boy's balaclava.

'Let him go, Dread, or I'm taking you out,' Mr Lionheart boomed.

Dad Dread yelped and ran back into the Dreadcraft.

Danny's lungs burned and his legs shook. He put his hands on his knees and tried to get his breath back. When he looked up, Crystallina was standing in front of him.

'Oh, hello.'

She beamed. 'Thank you, Da—,' she said. 'Sorry, I mean, Minor Boy.'

Danny shuffled from foot to foot. 'Aw, it was nothing, just doing my thing, you know.'

Crystallina sprang forward and gave him a hug so

tight that it bruised his ribs. 'For an evil super-villain, you're all right.'

'That's the sweetest thing I've EVER HEARD,' said Earl, muffled between them in Danny's pocket.

Crystallina reached into her belt and pulled out another communicator. 'Be more careful with this one, OK?'

Danny glanced up at the ship. Mr and Mrs Lionheart hovered above, looking confused.

He took the L in his hand and squeezed it. 'Promise.'

'Anyway, thanks again,' Crystallina said. 'And thanks to your rat and your bird.'

Earl popped out and curtsied. 'At your SERVICE!'

Crystallina smiled, then leaned over and gave Danny a peck on the balaclava. 'See you around,' she said.

Danny held his cheek and babbled something nonsensical about how if rats and pelicans can be friends then so can heroes and villains, but Mr Lionheart interrupted him.

'Hey, stop talking to that weird bird-kid, and freeze the ship!'

Crystallina sighed. Even through Danny's balaclava, she could tell he was scared. She winked at him, then turned back to her parents.

'My shades aren't working!' she yelled.

'WHAT?' Mr Lionheart cried.

The Dreadcraft lifted off the roof and zoomed away, leaving the Lionhearts, and Danny, stranded.

Crystallina pressed a button on her belt and within five seconds, a blue boomerang-shaped craft was hovering above them.

'Everybody huddle,' she said.

Danny awkwardly held Crystallina around the waist with one arm and the pelican with his other. 'What are you doing?' Mr Lionheart cried.

Crystallina pretended she couldn't hear him and pressed another button, which sent a line down. She grabbed it and in an instant, they were all zooming up into the craft.

'What's happening?' said Danny.

'I'm taking you home,' she said, leading them into the cockpit and strapping herself in.

'B-but . . .'

'Look, we both know you're not going to leave him,' she said. 'I mean, yes, every dad is annoying at times.' She nodded out of the window at her own furious father. 'But they're the only one you'll ever have.'

She hammered the Lionheart plane's booster and zoomed away, leaving her parents behind.

'All right,' said Danny. 'But can we make a detour on the way?'

Chapter Fifty-Five

'This craft can get you anywhere in the world within the hour,' said Crystallina, piloting the ship as if it was nothing. 'And we visited a TIP?'

Earl sat on a seat at the back, his belly full to breaking point. 'Uhhhhh, this has been the best day EVER.'

'Well, he's earned it,' said Danny.

When they got to within a couple of miles of the lair, they stopped. Danny didn't want to risk his dad seeing him being dropped off by a Lionheart.

'Thanks again, Danny,' said Crystallina.

'It's OK,' said Danny. 'Thank you for bringing us home. Aren't you going to get in trouble with your dad, though?'

She shrugged. 'He'll sulk for a bit, like he always does when a baddy gets away, but he'll snap out of it.'

Danny chuckled to himself. All this time he wanted to be more like Crystallina and they were basically the same person.

Danny and Earl said their goodbyes and climbed back on to the pelican for the rest of the journey.

He steered the pelican to the bottom of the cliff. He

DREAD
ENTERPRISES

didn't want to risk Dad recognizing it. Then, with Earl in his pocket, he climbed the rusty ladder to the lair entrance.

'Who'd have thunk it?' said Earl as they climbed. 'This whole time all that pelican wanted was a hug.'

Danny wasn't so sure about that, but he wasn't about to ruin the illusion.

They crept back into the lair. Danny removed his Mynah Boy costume and stashed it deep inside a hole in the cliff.

The Dreadcraft was parked diagonally across the bay. A huge chunk of roof lay smashed on the floor.

'Dad?' Danny called gingerly. 'Are you here?'

Dad Dread poked his head around the corner, his eyes ringed with red blotches. Oh no. He knows.

Dad's face slowly broke into a smile. 'Oh, Danny, you're OK!'

He ran over to him and scooped Danny up in his arms, kissing his forehead.

'OK, yep. Thanks.' Officially, Danny was embarrassed, but he was ecstatic that his dad was safe.

'My boy, I read Malevolo's file on the computer—I thought he'd killed you!'

Danny shrugged. 'He tried . . . I was too evil for him.'

Dad hopped and yelped. 'Ah, yes! What happened?'

Danny told Dad the full story. Well, apart from the whole Mynah Boy thing, of course. He told him how he had discovered Malevolo's treachery and that he built and piloted his own plane to stop him. He also told him that the so-called genius Malevolo blew himself up.

Dad danced around the lab like a delirious bunny. 'My boy built his own craft AND took out a threat to super-villainy everywhere, all in one day? And that Academy has the gall to call you a failure? Pah! They have no idea what they are talking about! Where is your craft now?'

'It's um, a bit . . . crashed,' said Danny.

Dad stopped dancing. 'Well, never mind,' he said. 'Not every great engineer can be a great pilot. The point is, you are alive and well and the Dread dynasty lives to fight another day!'

Danny half-smiled. He felt bad about lying, but he knew that this was how it was going to have to be. Dad could never know the truth about Mynah Boy.

Chapter Fifty-Six

It was the last day of the holidays. Even though this summer had been far more stressful than any school term, he was still sad. He was going to miss his friend.

'Don't worry about me, Danny,' said Earl as Danny packed his case. 'Us rats always find something to do. Have you ever seen a bored rat?'

'Well, yes. . . you, whenever I go on about Crystallina Lionheart.'

'Oh, yeah,' said Earl.

Danny stuffed his textbooks back into his bag. 'Can't you come with me?'

Earl's rat ears went down. 'You know I can't, Danny.'

'I suppose,' said Danny. 'It's just I get, I get . . .'

He wanted to say 'lonely' but couldn't bring himself to admit it.

'I know,' said Earl. 'But I'm not allowed at the Academy. And if they found me, can you imagine the experiments those CRAZY professors would do on me? Plus—' He stopped and looked around. 'Someone's got to stay here and keep an eye on your old man.'

Danny sighed. 'I know,' he said. 'I'll just, you know,

miss you and all that stuff.'

Earl smiled, his little teeth glinting in the light. 'That's why I made you this.'

He scurried under the bed and brought out two yellow metal Ms, each with their own button.

'What are they?'

'These are Mynah Communicators,' said Earl. 'If I need you, all I have to do is press this button. And vice versa.'

Danny held his M and watched the light glint off it. 'How did you do this?'

'I learned from the best,' said Earl.

Danny smiled. 'Thanks, Earl.' He held out his hand. 'Put it there.'

Earl looked at Danny's hand, then grabbed it in a huge hug. Danny patted him on the ear.

'Good luck at school, Danny,' said Earl. 'You'll be BRILLIANT.'

'And good luck here,' said Danny. 'I think you're going to need it.' He nodded at the window, where the pelican sat watching.

Earl laughed. 'I think the two of us are going to have some FUN.'

Chapter Fifty-Seven

The journey back to the Academy was much quicker when Dad and Danny weren't having to pedal. When they landed, Dad killed the Dreadcraft's engines and sighed.

'What's the matter?' said Danny.

Dad shook his head. 'This was supposed to be our moment of glory,' he said. 'We were going to walk in there and show them we weren't to be written off. But what have we achieved? Nothing.'

Danny wanted to talk Dad out of his funk but he couldn't think of anything to say. He was right, they hadn't taken over the world. He wasn't about to admit that it was his fault, though.

They walked under the rusty portcullis into the main hall. The Explosos stood there with the Blackhearts and the Trenchfoots. Dad tried to creep past unnoticed.

'Oh, Dread!' Ralfus Exploso called after him.

Dad screwed his eyes shut, stopped, and turned around. 'What is it, Exploso?'

Ralfus Exploso smoothed down his hair with a tiny hand and smirked. 'What happened to the big scheme?

I thought you were going to show all of us.'

The Blackhearts and the Trenchfoots laughed and jeered.

'All talk, no action. That's Dread all over.'

'Yeah, what a moron!'

'Hey, shut up!'

They stopped laughing and stared at Danny. 'Excuse me?' said Exploso.

'You heard me,' said Danny. 'You can't criticize my dad. All you managed to do was get busted by the Lionhearts. At least Dad NEARLY took over the world.'

The Explosos murmured something and stared at the floor.

Dad beamed with pride. 'Thanks, son,' he said, as they walked down the corridor.

'No problem,' said Danny.

As they passed the Wall of Fame, Phileas Dread piped up, 'Oh there they are—my pathetic son and my equally pathetic grandson. You make me ashamed to be a Dread.'

Without a word, Dad reached up and turned Phileas so he was facing the wall.

'Hey!' he called after them. 'You can't do that to me! I am Phileas Dread—conqueror of civilizations, master of fear.'

'Head in a bowl,' said Danny.

Dad and Danny looked at each other and burst out laughing.

They were nearly at Danny's dorm when a dark shadow passed in front of them.

'Welcome back, Mr Dread,' said Dame Demento.

'Ahhhh, hello, ma'am,' Dad half-squealed.

'I have watched your antics with interest over the summer,' she said. 'And I must applaud your effort. However, at no point did I see Danny helping. Why was that?'

Danny didn't know what to say. Because I'm not really evil? Because I spent the whole summer secretly foiling his evil plans?

Dad Dread put his hand on his son's shoulder. 'Danny is responsible for stopping the man who took out the Destructors, the Cerberians, and the Pillagers.'

Dame Demento's terrifying green eyes opened wide. 'Really?'

They nodded.

'But the League of Evil had been trying to track him down for years.'

Danny shrugged. 'Maybe they were going about it the wrong way.'

Dame Demento allowed a tiny smile to play on her lips.

'Hmm, maybe I underestimated you, young Dread. It will be interesting to observe your progress this term.'

After Dad left, Danny settled back into his dorm. He took out both of his communicators and placed them in his secret box along with his Mynah Boy costume.

He just about managed to hide it when the Mayhem twins burst in.

'DANNY!' Murray yelled. 'How was your summer ours was amazing we tried to make loads of giant sheep but this really crappy Italian superhero stopped us and then he saved the world on the telly and we were all like **HOW DID HE GET SO GOOD** and we've still got that giant fly.'

He stopped and tried to get his breath back.

'Well, that was our summer,' said Matt. 'What did you get up to?'

Danny shrugged. 'Not much. Met a talking rat, you know, the usual.'

When the Mayhems left to find some sugar for their super fly, Danny sat down on his bed and stuck a new cutting into his secret book.

PLOT TO DESTROY CIVILIZATION FOILED BY MINOR BOY

Citizens of the world united in relief yesterday after a mysterious new superhero foiled a dastardly plot at the World Peace Summit to start World War Three and eliminate crime-fighting family, the Lionhearts.

'Without Minor Boy's help, we would have been done for, and the world as we know it would have been over. We'd like to thank him for everything,' said Crystallina.

When pressed to elaborate about the identity of 'Minor Boy', with whom she had been seen sharing an embrace and escaping in her plane, Crystallina told our reporter to 'push off'.

Danny smiled as he read the story for the fiftieth time. Suddenly, school didn't seem so bad. If the past summer had taught him anything, it was that he could use all the evil skills he had learnt there and apply them to good. And no matter what happened, no matter how much Rufus Exploso mocked him, or how harshly his teachers berated him, the one thing that would get him through was his big secret.

Danny Dread had saved the world.

As well as writing books, Ben Davis has had a variety of jobs, including radio joke writer, library assistant, and postman. Writing books has proven the most fun.

Ben resides in Tamworth, Staffordshire, with his wife and a big wimpy dog called Tommy. They currently live in a small terraced house, but Ben is saving up for his own mountain lair.

Find out more about Ben at the
Not So Private Blog of Ben Davis:
bendavisauthor.blogspot.co.uk

You can also visit his website:
bendavisauthor.com